Eastern Ambitions

Compass Brothers, Book 3

Jayne Rylon and Mari Carr

ISBN: 978-1-941785-49-2

Editor: Amy Sherwood

Cover Artist: Jayne Rylon

Print Formatting: Mari Carr

He's lost everything. Can he win her heart?

Sam Compton never liked getting his hands dirty, at least not on Compass Ranch. Armed with a business degree, he's about to become the youngest VP at an illustrious Wall Street investment firm. Until his partner in an office romance turns into an ultra-refined snake in the grass.

Staggering from the punch of betrayal, another blow threatens to level him. His father is dying. He races home to lend his brain to his brothers' backs at the ranch, and finds something he never expected. A sophisticated yet playful woman stimulates his mind...and parts below the belt.

Compass Ranch gave Cindi Middleton's wounded soul everything it needs: a home, acceptance, and respect—not to mention unlimited sex—from the ranch's sexy cowboys. Despite their instant and intense sparks, Sam's defection to the bright city lights she left behind is a big red flag. She's been there, done that, burned the T-shirt.

Yet the heat of their attraction brings them circling back to each other's arms...until a certain snake reappears, threatening to endanger the acquisition of the one thing Sam has realized is truly priceless.

Warning: Tissue alert! The authors recommend you have a few on hand while reading this book. To make up for any sniffles, a host of cowboys with open arms await to console you, distract you or make your wildest dreams come true.

Dedication

For all the people in our lives—and those of our readers—who have fought cancer and won. We also remember those who've lost the battle. The circle of impacted lives encompasses so many more than those who have the disease. Our hearts go out to caretakers, partners, neighbors, family and friends too.

In Honor Of
Anne Rainey's Mom
Grammie
Janette Anneken
Jeannette
Jenn Matthis
Jennifer Haymore
Johanna Snodgrass

In Memory Of
Annie
Bianca D'Arc's Mom
Grandma Gretchen
Aunt Loretta
Grandma Mary
Uncle Bill
Uncle Vinny
Aunt Rose

One Goal: End Cancer - http://www.pelotonia.org

Prologue

Sam Compton rocked on his heels as his twin, Sawyer, waved goodbye to their father. Shitty speakers and awful acoustics beneath the tin portico protecting the drop-off lane at the airport garbled shrill flight announcements.

The racket disguised the rasp of Sam clearing the knot from his throat as his brother jammed his hands in his pockets and sighed. Sawyer hitched his duffle higher when it slipped from his slumped shoulders.

Sam winced. If Sawyer's back ached as badly as his, that had to hurt like a bitch. He needed something to take his mind off the pain—both the sting between his shoulder blades and the disturbing ache residing somewhat deeper in his chest.

Sawyer squinted at the vanishing taillights of the ranch's pickup.

"Guess that's that." Sam angled toward the automatic doors leading to the terminal. His twin followed as though he were a reflection in a mirror instead of a separate human being. It was only right that they leave together even if they were heading in opposite directions.

All their lives, they'd been so much the same while ultimately completely different. It figured they'd only discovered how strong their bond could be shortly before sacrificing it for their futures.

Dreams of attending college had sprouted in Sam long before Sawyer had kicked Roger Latner's ass, for teasing them about their ranch family's *ignorance*, in the third grade. No one had laughed once they grew old enough to realize how much power the Comptons— especially JD—wielded in their Wyoming town, Compton Pass. Most of their friends would have killed to be one of the infamous Compass Brothers, yet every one of the four—starting with Silas—had left home the moment they'd turned eighteen.

Probably had something to do with their frontiersmen genes, which urged them to blaze their own paths and create their own kingdoms instead of ruling a hand-me-down legacy. Pride was never in short supply in their pastures.

Still, the look in his mother's eyes as she'd surrendered her youngest...

"Gotta admit we were lucky JD talked Mom into staying behind or we'd still be standing on that curb out there." Sawyer's usual permagrin chased away some of their gloom.

"No shit. As it was, I thought she might crack a few ribs during that never-ending goodbye at home." Sam would miss sharing this wavelength with Sawyer. He'd never once been lonely in his entire life. Between his crazy-ass older brothers, the ranch hands, JD and Vicky plus his twin, he'd hardly had a thought he didn't share.

What would it be like to live in silence?

His back throbbed. The giant compass design there had been worn first by Silas. Now all four of the Compass Brothers bore their own brand of home. Each with unique flair. Sam smiled as he recalled the ornate E on the frame enclosing a mural of their spread. No matter where he roamed, Compass Ranch would remain the center of his universe.

The scrollwork and intricate lines comprising the script of his cardinal direction reminded him of the illuminated dropped capitals featured on the Learning Channel's special about the Book of Kells and other ancient tomes. Maybe someday, when the blaze dulled to something less than this raging irritation, he'd enjoy the damn thing.

"My back is on fucking fire." Sawyer flexed his shoulders.

If JD had caught the twins getting matching, massive tattoos from Snake—the same cowboy-turned-artist who'd inked their brothers when each had come of age—it would have been more than skin-deep discomfort making their plane rides awkward. Still, Sam suspected even if he'd whopped their asses like he had the time he busted them stealing a case of beer from his employees' bunkhouse, their old man would have been proud.

Maybe grateful they hadn't abandoned everything and everyone who loved them.

Sam glanced at his watch. He'd typed up a master schedule of his flight numbers, departure times, trip duration and connecting gates, then arranged the info in a three ring binder along with maps from La Guardia to his residence hall at Columbia. Sections had smudged from his frequent handling. He'd studied the notes enough to have the worn bits memorized.

An hour and twenty-seven minutes should be plenty to make it through security and share one last drink with his brother. "Looks like we made good time. What do you say we check our bags and then hit the bar until take-off?"

Sawyer laughed. "We're eighteen, Mr. Hotshit. They're not going to serve us."

Sounded like a challenge to Sam. One-upping

dares had landed them in tons of trouble over the years. Why should this be any different? "I bet I can charm us into a couple of microbrews. Especially if the bartender is a college girl."

"Make mine a Miller Lite."

There was no accounting for his brother's taste. Sam couldn't wait to surround himself with culture, education and class. People who relied on their brains instead of blisters for their living. Sawyer had always wallowed in the down and dirty while Sam had clawed his way out of the muck.

As though Sawyer could read Sam's thoughts, he took a swipe at his brother, smacking him in the gut with the back of his knuckles. "Besides, who's gonna be smart enough to hit the books but dumb enough to forget to card your scrawny ass?"

Ouch. This past summer Sawyer *had* bulked up. Sam made a mental note to check out the fitness center he'd spied on the school's website. Ranchers didn't have to rely on slick machinery in air-conditioned buildings to stay in shape. Without his chores... Well, he wouldn't mind if girls drooled over him like they had over Sawyer lately.

Afternoons splashing around at the local swimming hole had netted them both plenty of stolen kisses. But Sawyer had nearly drowned in female attention. The jerk.

"Really, Sawyer? How many times have I explained why insulting your twin is ridiculous?" Sam faked a pretentious laugh as he shook his head.

"Hey, not my fault you spent all your time studying instead of working out in the barn."

"Are you referring to bucking hay or bucking Beth while her dad rode herd with JD?"

"Take your pick." Sawyer rubbed his flat abs and sighed. A shit-eating grin highlighted the dimples they both had hated when they were younger. His brother hadn't hesitated to add them to his hottie-hunting arsenal as soon as he realized how effective they were. "We may have started out identical. Now I can kick your ass."

"Probably could if you were smart enough to catch me, baby brother." Okay, so Sam was only a few minutes older. Never hurt to remind the runt he was littlest, though. "I still say we should have taken Snake up on his offer to make us identification."

"How are you gonna survive without me?" Sawyer had never made the grades Sam did. He did have a knack for conjuring luck and surfing his instincts through tricky situations. "Those fake IDs of his look like shit. We'd have been busted the first time we tried to use them, and JD would have kicked our asses."

"Fine, chicken. I won't tell if you indulge in one last watermelon fizz." Sam ambled toward the ticket counter. To tell the truth, he wouldn't mind a shot of something sweet either. If his brother went for it he could chalk up the childish indulgence to sentiment.

He dealt with the agent, supplying each piece of data before she requested it. With his license out and ready, he watched her input something off the card. A clatter followed as she banged on the ancient keyboard. Why exactly it took her roughly four million keystrokes to verify his information remained a cosmic mystery. After all, he was pretty sure she could have launched a space shuttle with all those clicks.

A cough rasped through his throat, which dried out as they dropped off their baggage and passed through security. Counting down the seconds to escape from rural, small-town life had somehow never registered as a ticking time bomb about to obliterate his bond with his twin.

Sawyer dove into the first bar past the scanners

and plopped onto a stool. Sam would have preferred to locate their gates and sit closest to the departure point, just in case, but he let it slide. No sense in spending their final time together arguing. A pretty waitress dropped off a pair of sodas.

"At least we'll be on the same coast for a bit." Sawyer played with the condensation on his glass. "Cape May's not all that far from New York City."

"You'll be in basic training for eight weeks. And then the Coast Guard will station you God knows where. Doesn't matter how damn close the cities are, it's not like we're going to be hanging out together." Sam was glad his portfolio, funded with birthday and Christmas money, had performed well enough to buy them both decent laptops without having to bug their parents to spring for them. Maybe next year, after he started his finance classes, he would ramp up his trading. To guarantee he could keep in touch with Sawyer, he'd pulled the trigger on riskier investments than he would have preferred.

They wouldn't share the new discoveries waiting in the worlds they'd chosen side by side. At least they could email and use the new service he'd read about, Skype, if their schedules ever lined up. Maybe they could even teach Silas and Seth how to join in.

"I get ten days leave after basic. I'll come check out your fine preppy institution in New York before I ship off."

"More like you'll raid the coed dorms before you're forced to spend months in barracks with a bunch of dudes." Not that the sleeping arrangements would stop Sawyer. Growing up on the ranch they'd learned all kinds of strategies from the hands, who had devised a naughty playbook to liven up the evenings. Sneaking girls in to share, finding shadowy spots in the barn for some privacy, a midnight jaunt to the local bar... The cowboys never suffered a shortage of the horizontal two-step despite their close quarters. Sam sort of regretted not being able to employ some of the veterans' tag-team tactics with his twin.

"Yeah well, I've waited a long time to use the I'm-leaving-in-the-morning-give-me-something-to-remember line." Sawyer twisted his face into a pitiful mask. His wide eyes and crimped brows probably would compel droves of women to comfort the sneaky bastard.

"You've seen *Band of Brothers* one too many times, Saw."

"Whatever. No shitting, though, it'd be cool to see the Statue of Liberty."

At least they agreed on that. Sam couldn't wait to explore the monuments and museums of NYC. He'd watched his share of *Law & Order* and *The Real World Manhattan* when he'd wrestled the remote to the TV in their room from Sawyer. "I'll take you around the city. We'll hit the clubs and I'll show you all the fun we've been missing in Bumfuck."

Sam had argued the grass was greener in the big city ever since he'd applied to the single university, Ivy League Columbia, he was determined to attend. JD pointed out nothing grew in the concrete landscape where Sam was headed. Sam had shaken off the morose thought and imagined standing in front of the famous Egyptian Temple of Dendur in the sunroom at the Met and what it would be like to chow down a hotdog in the stands at Yankee Stadium.

When no one spied on him, he'd scooped up a bottleful of the Wyoming dirt and tucked it in his new suitcase next to his digital photoframe—loaded with snapshots of his brothers—and wrapped it in his favorite T-shirt, which Silas had mailed home from Alaska his first Christmas absent from Compass Ranch.

How could that have been three years ago already?

Sawyer chuckled before turning serious. "I can't wait. Look, Sam…"

"Last call for passenger Compton." A choppy crackle blasted through the elevator music in the airport lounge. "Please proceed to gate 5A. This will serve as the final boarding call for Flight 328 to Atlantic City."

"What the—" Sawyer bolted to his feet, digging in his Levi's for his boarding pass.

With one hand, Sam saved the seat his brother had occupied from crashing to the floor. Not only had he committed his schedule to memory weeks ago, but he'd also badgered Sawyer until the dumbass had looked up his stuff late last night. "I thought your plane left at 3:30?"

"Shit!" Sawyer double-checked the info. "That must have been the flight number. Three twenty-eight. It's scheduled for 3 o'clock."

"You better run." Sam shoved Sawyer toward the door instead of smothering him in another hug guaranteed to send spikes down his spine. Sam didn't even clap him on the shoulder in a more manly display. "It's already five after."

"But…" For the first time, Sawyer looked like the youngest Compton. He stumbled as he crossed the line between the tile of the bar and the industrial carpet of the main thoroughfare.

"Go!" Sam shooed his twin, then spun toward the waitress. Without glancing at his brother—who froze, biting his lip—he snagged the young lady gently by the wrist and smiled when she didn't yank free. "Would you mind paging the airline for us? Let them know passenger Sawyer Compton, C-O-M-P-T-O-N is en route for Flight 328."

"Sure thing, sugar." She smiled slow and wide. "If I can take his place while you finish your drink."

"Sounds great." He winked and groaned inside where normally he'd have done a big mental fist pump. Because Sawyer still hovered on the edge of Sam's peripheral vision. He flung his arms out wide. "What are you waiting for?"

"I don't know." Sawyer swallowed hard enough Sam saw his throat flex from ten feet away. "You'll email, right?"

Shit. If Sawyer bailed now, Sam could never go through with his own desertion.

"Promise. Every day. I'll write you so many letters, I'll put Lucy to shame." Sam grinned as he thought of the sweet woman engaged to his father's best ranch hand. She'd carried her notebook everywhere these past three years, keeping Silas in the loop on the activity at home. Sam had always wondered... "How else will I make you jealous over all the ladies on campus?"

"They're waiting for you, cowboy." The waitress flashed a smile worthy of a toothpaste commercial. She pointed. "Head that direction, to the very end of the concourse. They said they'll give you five and then you're out of luck. You look like you can make it."

She checked out the lean muscle of Sawyer's build in a not-so-subtle sweep.

"You *will* make it." Sam nodded as Sawyer took one step, then another, picking up speed.

"So will you." Sawyer grinned over his shoulder before sprinting down the hall.

"Thank you." Sam held the chair out for the waitress. "Still care to join—"

A giant bellow caught them both off guard. "Compass Brothers rule!"

Sawyer's battle cry faded.

Sam couldn't help but smirk.

"He can say that again." The waitress giggled.

13

"Two guys like you should be illegal. How long before *your* flight?"

"Have to be at the gate in twenty minutes." Tension in his hand melted beneath her stroking fingers, which roamed over his knuckles.

"I have a break. Let me tell my manager I plan to use it, and I'll help you forget all about those jitters. Give you something to send you off in style, huh?" Her hand squeezed his knee beneath the slightly sticky table.

"That's not necessary." Sam swallowed a glug of soda and coughed.

Her roaming hand cupped him. "It's my pleasure."

Oh man, Sawyer would be greener than the Hulk when he read the first installment of their perpetual email chain, which Sam would start tonight.

Chapter One

Seven Years Later

"You should have seen them. Smoking hot quadruplets, Sam." Sawyer bragged about his most recent conquest to Seth and Sam over the open videoconference link while they waited for Silas to join in the call. "Two for you, two for me."

"Sawyer Compton, what kind of trouble are you getting into now?" Vicky, their mom, laughed at the horror on her youngest son's face when she popped into the last quadrant on the screen. Silas had returned to Compass Ranch. Too bad his trip had been courtesy of an oil rig explosion that had nearly killed the tough son of a bitch.

"Dude, a little warning would have been nice before you tossed Mom on the line." To see the Coastie blush made Sam's day. Even better was the hazy image of Silas in the background, looking mostly in one piece. His leg would be jacked for months, maybe forever. Otherwise, he'd recover. Funny how hearing the news hadn't convinced Sam as much as that one glimpse of home and his family out west.

Four pictures divided his screen. He'd placed the images of his brothers as they were situated around the country. His window on the right. Sawyer—in San Francisco—on the left, Silas—home from Alaska—on the top and Seth—in Texas—at the bottom.

"Hello, my sons." Vicky tried a little finger wave, giggling at the reflection of herself on the screen.

"Hi, Mom." They answered her together.

"All right, I see I'm crashing this party. Just wanted to see my boys a second. Have fun and call me soon. I love you."

A chorus of "Love you too" echoed through the state-of-the-art conference equipment in Sam's high-rise office. He steepled his fingers and waited.

The snick of a door closing bounced off his glass desktop and the floor-to-ceiling windows overlooking the Manhattan skyline before Silas announced, "Okay, she's out."

"How much of that did she hear?" Sawyer adjusted his uniform. He must be on a dinner break. It was nearly quitting time for Sam despite his ridiculous hours. If it weren't for his ten o'clock dinner with Belinda, he might have stayed past midnight again.

The promise of some extra-sweet dessert, assuming he could negotiate the merger he'd been considering for a while, lured him from his workaholic tendencies.

"Obviously I missed a good story." Si let Sawyer off the hook. "Nothing but the last few words came across. You're clear."

"Holy shit, I almost had a heart attack." Sawyer clutched his chest. Served him right for gloating.

"You know, her and JD aren't exactly prudes." Seth—kicked back in jeans and no shirt with a beer in hand after a long hard day—supplied some dirt. "I heard from Jim Spade they tore it up back in the day.

Plus, remember the time Sam walked in on them in the kitchen?"

"Gross. I could have gone my whole life without thinking about that again, fuckwad." Sam adjusted the sleeves of his Burberry shirt to keep them from wrinkling any worse. At least his suit coat hung neatly from the rack in the corner. He focused on a vision of Belinda in the slinky designer dress she'd promised to debut for him later to erase the lingering horror of JD and Vicky's overwhelming passion. If they weren't his parents, he'd have been impressed.

Ack.

Belinda. Dress. Décolletage. Sexy legs. Superior intelligence. Future material.

That's better.

"Moving on…" Seth grinned for Silas. "How the hell are you, bro? You look surly as ever. The mountain man beard is a nice touch."

Jesus, he wasn't kidding. That thing would frighten a grizzly. Hell, maybe it had. Si had worked some rough places. The escalating danger his brother faced had given Sam more than one nightmare, not that he'd admit it now that Si was safe at Compass Ranch.

"Better today than yesterday." Silas seemed to note the real concern beneath the teasing. As the oldest brother, he'd always been the one to look after them, not the other way around. "Can't wait to get out of this bed. Maybe take Rainey for a ride."

Sam couldn't believe their father had taken care of their horses all this time. The high-quality animals would have brought him a neat profit if he'd auctioned them off. JD never let go. Some part of Sam was glad. He would love the wind in his face as he moved in sync with Dee, flying over the terrain they'd learned together a lifetime ago. If only he could scrounge some time.

"Why not stay there? Give Lucy a go, instead.

Hell of a lot more fun than a middle-aged horse."
Sawyer broke the tension, wringing a laugh from Sam.
No one else joined in. "Oh, fuck. Too soon?"

"Moron." Seth shook his head.

Silas growled. "Don't talk about her like that.
She's married."

Sam had to try really hard not to roll his eyes
since it wouldn't be becoming of the Director of
Commodity Trading at Smith, Winfield and Gandle.

"To a man who wants you just as bad as she
does." Sawyer didn't zip his mouth despite a glare from
Seth. Good for him. *Tell it like it is, Saw.* "How long
are we gonna pretend we don't notice them begging for
scraps of information from us? How many times are we
gonna let Silas fuck things up? One of these days it'll
be too late. If I had that kind of love in my life, I sure as
shit wouldn't waste it."

Identical twins, identical logic—at least this time.
Sam understood where Sawyer was coming from. Lucy
and Colby *had* made something together. Something
pretty fucking great by all accounts. Colby had
flourished as the ranch's foreman, and Lucy had a
waiting list of clients a mile long for her nursing
practice focused on homebound patients. And yet,
anyone who knew them well could tell something was
missing. Someone gimping around Wyoming with one
good leg and a hell of a lot of apologizing to do.

"It doesn't freak you guys out? The whole Colby
thing?" Silas had never talked directly with them about
his bisexuality, though Sam and Sawyer had often
speculated about their brother's relationship with his
best friends. How could they not? No one kept the
flame alive as long as Lucy had without a deeper
connection than surviving sloppy-joe day in the high
school cafeteria or suffering through four years of
Spanish together.

On top of that, both Sam and Sawyer had picked up some decidedly non-platonic vibes from Silas's last roommate, Red. Damn, when they'd heard the man had died in the accident that'd injured his brother, things had really sunk in. So close…

Sam debated how best to express his acceptance when Seth beat him to it. "I don't care to know the play by play, but who you fuck is your business."

Sawyer and Seth both nodded in agreement.

"If I can stand to listen to Sawyer go on about his whips and chains, I think I can handle you getting moony over a guy we all respect."

Sam grinned at that. Who said *moony* anymore, anyway? Only Seth with his good-ole-boy charm could pull it off and not sound like a total tool.

"I think it's kind of hot." Sawyer shrugged. They all knew of his penchant for BDSM. Power games appealed to their youngest brother. "Not my thing exactly, but I can see how having another guy submit would be a turn-on."

Sam choked. He hadn't imagined things to the same level of X-rated detail as Saw obviously had.

"Don't act like you've never shared a woman with another dude, Sam. I know you have. And you liked it."

That might have been the understatement of the century.

"Sawyer—" When would the little fucker learn that sometimes secrets were secrets? Even from their older brothers. What would the guys say if they found out about the dirty habits he'd picked up from frat parties at Columbia? Or refined at the ultra-elite fetish clubs he'd frequented since then?

He hoped they'd understand.

Besides, his brothers were one thing. Referring to orgies while he sat here, in his immaculate office, was another. Thank God those establishments had excessive privacy policies. He refused to jeopardize his standing at S, W & G to indulge his darker urges. Too many people were judgmental of things they didn't understand. And few would approve of his need to share and show off.

"No, the kid's right." Silas cut into Sam's drifting thoughts. He shrugged when all three of his brothers stared, speechless. "I've done a lot of thinking lately. More today."

He grabbed a handful of crumpled envelopes and let them rain around him. "I'm not going to hide who I am anymore."

"You read her letters." Sam had to scale down the brightness on the screen. His eyes bulged as he scoured the image of Silas's surroundings.

"Holy shit." Seth dropped his feet off his desk, leaning closer to his monitor for a better look at the background. "They're everywhere."

"What was in them?" Sawyer had always been curious. He'd often mentioned the letters to Sam. "I can't tell you how many Christmases, Thanksgivings and nights I spent on leave I'd see little Lucy huddled with a pad and a pen, writing away like mad. She never let me peek, though. What did she tell you?"

"Everything." Silas grimaced when his voice cracked a bit. "It's the best gift I could have imagined. A time machine. Every bit of the ten years I missed, it's all here. There were even some pictures."

He held up a few snapshots for his brothers to check out.

"Ohhh, did she include good bits too?" Sam had always thought his oldest brother's friend was smoking. Beneath the goody-two-shoes exterior there lurked a naughty girl. He'd wager his whole pile of Google stock on it. Even the shares he'd picked up in his freshman year at Columbia from the IPO. He wiggled his brows. "Nasty stuff?"

Silas chose not to indulge Sam's prying. He didn't deny it either.

"Damn! She *did* write about that stuff. Look at his face."

Before Silas could tell them to fuck off, a distraction took the heat from his revelation.

A sassy voice called out from somewhere, "Tell your brothers it's not nice to kiss and tell. Well, I suppose this Lucy did but sharing a note with a lover is different than tossing those fantasies to a pack of rabid, ungrateful, fickle cowboys."

"Who the hell was that?" Sawyer jumped at the rebuke.

"Only the cowgirl your fucking asshole brother is keeping prisoner in this god forsaken shack. Will someone please call 911?"

Seth grinned into the camera before tossing over his shoulder, "Don't make me gag you, darlin'."

"Holy shit." Sam scooted his chair so tight to his desk the arms wedged beneath the surface, caging him in. Could it be? "What is that in the background? Do I see pretty ankles tied to the end of your bed, Seth?"

"I'm Jody Kirkland. My dad is your brother's boss. He'll probably also be the man to murder this piece of shit, arrogant, limp dick when he finds out what he's up to."

"I'll give you arrogant, but I'm guessing Seth's anything but a limp dick right now, honey." Sam braved his brother's wrath because just looking at those red-tipped toes had him shifting his cock to make room in his slacks. Life with these three around would never be boring. God, how he missed spending time with them.

"Argh! You're all alike. I can't believe there are

really *four* of you. Thank God you spread yourselves out. No state should have to house that many Compass Brothers. Especially if you're all as dense as Seth."

"I like this girl." Sawyer met Sam's eyes through the fiber optics and miles between them. They laughed together.

"So you're calling the police?" Legs thrashed at the corner of the mattress.

"I don't think my mom would appreciate Seth missing out on the next ten Christmases because he's in jail." Sawyer winked at his brothers. "Sorry, honey. You know, I bet he could help you make the most of the situation."

"You're all bastards. Every one of you asshats."

She might have been right. Sam had thought a lot lately about his future. With the VP position within reach and a woman he got more serious about every day, he wondered what it would be like to build a life only to have his someday children wash their hands of it all—thumb their noses at his hard work. Maybe he'd make a point of visiting Compass Ranch.

Sometime.

After this next presentation.

And the one after that. And—

"Jody. Give me two minutes. Then we'll talk, okay?" Seth's exasperated groan spoke volumes. Maybe more than one Compton had found their mate. Who else could drive them this nuts? "Look, Si. I swear I thought I'd crapped my pants when they told me you'd almost gotten blown up. So I'm going to say this flat out. I know you're still on the mend but ignoring what Lucy and Colby are offering would be ridiculous."

Sam agreed. The golden chance at happiness was valuable beyond price. Something he didn't say often. As he neared the pinnacle, his dreams started to seem a little less lofty. Money, power, work… All they seemed to lead to was more responsibility. Loosening his tie, he debated reaching for the jumbo bottle of Tums in his bottom drawer. Lately…

He shook his head. No, he'd gunned for this for years. Tonight he'd relax with Belinda and regroup. He had to focus now more than ever. If he was tired, who could blame him?

"Says the man talking to his brothers instead of playing with the sexy woman tied to his bed about to escape." Silas cracked a full-on smile, something Sam hadn't seen in at least a decade.

He whipped his stare to Seth's quadrant on the large screen he used for international meetings. That was one scrumptious cowgirl. He felt fifteen again when he and his twin bombarded the line with whistles and catcalls.

"What!" Seth spun in his chair. When he spotted Jody—naked, in the camera's line of sight as she undid the last of the knots—the sight spurred him to action. He snagged a blanket off the foot of the bed, then wrapped it around her. "What the hell do you think you're doing?"

"Leaving, moron!" The filly thrashed in Seth's embrace until his brother hefted her over his shoulder, bundled in the blanket. Damn him for ruining the view.

"Okay, as fun as this is, I have to be on deck in five minutes." Sawyer grimaced. "Someone better fill me in later."

"No, there will be no filling in!" Seth marched to the camera, blocking it with his palm. "I have to go, Si. We'll talk more. Soon."

His connection terminated with a generic beep, leaving Sam and Silas alone on the line. They looked at each other and laughed.

"Almost time for me to hit the city, bro." Sam stretched, taking his suit coat from the hanger behind him. He'd chosen the navy blue because Belinda always seemed to purr when she saw him filling out its tailored lines. His gaze zipped past the bustle on the streets below him. Somehow the lights in the background didn't captivate him as they had the first time he'd stared into the sea of fallen stars.

"Hot date?"

"Sort of. Been spending some time with a girl I work with," he hedged. For some reason he hadn't shared Belinda with his brothers. Maybe because he'd always insisted on deflecting passes made by co-workers before. Another clue she was different. Special. "I think she's worth the risk."

"Trust your gut, Sam. I should have done the same a long time ago." His brother nodded. "If you're wrong, at least you'll know you tried."

Sam smiled. "I'm glad you're home. Safe."

"When are you coming to visit? It's not the same without you three around to piss me off."

"Too hard to fit in a trip. I'm up for VP, Si." Though he'd thought the same not five minutes before, he hated saying it aloud. How could he make Silas understand how close he was to achieving everything he'd slaved for? "I'd be the youngest in the history of the company."

"We all have our dreams, Sam." Silas wouldn't begrudge his brother a shot at his. "Good luck."

"You too." Sam smiled. "I think you're going to need it."

Chapter Two

Five days later, Sam tossed the keys to his Maserati Gran Turismo S to the valet. Driving in the city could be a bitch. Sliding behind the wheel of that sexy beast made it all worthwhile.

It would take more than epic traffic to irritate him after the progress he'd made this week. Usually standoffish, Belinda had encouraged him to share more of each evening with her. Time well spent. The refreshment had cleared his mind as she'd promised it would. Enough to convince him of the good sense in her suggestion to wrap his project before the last dinner reservation so they could blow off some steam together.

Though he'd struck out the night of his call with his brothers, and all week since, something in her naughty wink had given him hope. If it meant what he thought, he'd be relaxed enough to deliver the pitch of a lifetime tomorrow morning. His research was in the bag. Showing it off was the only step left.

"Should I leave it out front, sir?" The title from someone at least a dozen years older sat funny with Sam. What kind of assholes must the valet deal with every day? Rich bastards who assumed a man who worked for his living would be incompetent at his job.

"Nah. I trust you." He flipped a generous tip into the man's palm. "Do me a favor. Have some fun when you take her to the garage. She likes her legs stretched a bit now and then."

"Will do, sir." The man flashed a genuine smile that burned away the polite facsimile he'd sported flawlessly before. "Enjoy your meal."

"You bet I will." Sam wished he'd worn a hat to dip in the man's direction. Some habits died hard, not that he'd give in to the urge to sport a Stetson in public. Bad enough his accent had made a comeback lately. He'd practiced long and hard to eradicate the drawl from his pronunciations during that first interminable winter far from home.

With success came a measure of security. Less to prove meant he could relax his guard, at least a little. And that's when the flavor of Wyoming snuck in again. Oh, well. The partners had taken to calling him The Cowboy Trader. He sort of liked it, not that he'd admit it considering Belinda's instant repulsion to the *unrespectable* nickname.

What would she think of his tattoo? Hopefully he'd find out tonight. Why else would she have suggested they take time off at the very peak of the crunch? Only one person worked harder, suffering longer hours than he did, in their office. Belinda.

You have your presentation up here, Sam. She'd perched on the arm of his ridiculously expensive office chair to run her fingers through his hair. Christ, it'd given him daydreams of laying her out on his desk and damn the floor to ceiling windows. A major breakthrough. She *never* touched him at work. Careful, cautious, proper—Belinda paid close attention to the image she presented in the male-dominated arena.

What would she be like in bed? Maybe she'd turn

wild and release the hint of bad girl he'd sensed lurking inside her conservative shell like the delicious, gooey center of a strawberry candy. The artwork inked on his back could turn her on. Or maybe it'd be best to leave the lights down low and save that surprise for another time.

He smiled and checked his close-cropped hair in the reflection on the sparkling clean door before one of the staff tugged on the gleaming gold handle with his white-gloved hand. It opened smoothly, perfectly quiet. So different from the creaky hinge on the back porch of the ranch house. JD had always said leaving it noisy served him better. No one snuck in or out of their domain. With four teenaged boys, going stingy with the oil had probably been the right approach.

Heaven help you if you slammed the storm door, though. Vicky would go ballistic. He was still thinking of ancient history when yet another member of the high-performing team of restaurateurs led him to the best table—cozy, private and dashed with just enough candlelight to be romantic while preserving some shadows—in the exclusive prime steakhouse.

Best of all, the spot came complete with a gorgeous, refined woman to match.

"Well, now." Belinda accepted the lingering kiss he pressed to her pursed lips. She didn't often demonstrate affection in public. He could understand that, he supposed. "Isn't that a lovely smile?"

Probably best not to admit he'd been thinking of his mom.

"All for you." He frowned when he realized it'd likely be a few hours before he could check out the rest of her glamorous, red dress. Hopefully, as he peeled it from her inch by inch. The sweetheart neckline accentuated her full breasts without detracting from her propriety. Classic and understated, the platinum pendant with ruby accents he'd bought for her birthday nestled in the hollow of her throat. He planned to lick that spot later. It had been driving him mad for quite a while.

Not the kind of man to abstain for months on end, he'd reached the breaking point in their cat and mouse game. Tonight he could use a distraction—from his deadlines, tomorrow's make-or-break meeting and the terror that had shaken his foundation last week when he'd learned Silas had almost... On top of that, Seth had texted about a spur-of-the-moment trip home. Sam had spent damn near twenty minutes trying to connect with his older brother to learn more. He'd failed. Something didn't feel right, and it had him on edge. To hell with coy. He could use a sounding board. "I didn't mean to keep you waiting. My brother—"

Belinda waved him off with a flick of her French manicure before he could relate the whole chain of events. He sank into the seat with a sigh, eating his confession about Silas, the Lucy and Colby situation, Seth and his captive and the laughs he'd shared with Sawyer over his quadruplet bust before Seth's random visit to Wyoming. Silence made a bitter appetizer. Probably for the best. She wouldn't appreciate him showing his roots. Reminding her of the dirt he'd sprouted from could constitute poor foreplay strategy.

"Excuses aren't necessary, darling." Her saccharine tone didn't match the flash of her glare, which she attempted to veil with fluttering lashes.

Things had to go perfect here if he was to have a shot at convincing her to spend the night at his place. After that it'd be a small step to fusing their lives. Equals in business and partners at home. Someday soon she'd follow him up the corporate ladder. Hell, he'd thought for a while there she might beat him to the top and more power to her. He couldn't imagine a more ideal match even if she required some convincing. Luckily, he had a few tricks up his sleeve.

Expensive ones. Her favorite kind.

"Let me make it up to you, B." He'd been called charming by everyone from past girlfriends to the write-up *The Wall Street Journal* had done on fresh talent last year. Time to put his skills to good use.

"How do you plan to do that?" She canted her chin, allowing the flickering light to dance over her porcelain skin.

"I believe you're about to find out." Sam rested his shoulders on the tufted leather of the tall chair back and allowed the sommelier to present a peace offering.

"Madame." He slid a bottle along his towel-draped forearm, label side out. "Your gentleman has selected a rare delight for tonight's meal. An excellent choice."

"Oh, let me be the judge. What will you serve us?" She baited the man with a tiny flex of her lips.

"A Premier Grand Cru Classé Bordeaux from Chateau Pavie of Saint-Émilion. The 2000 vintage."

"Impressive." She traced one manicured nail along Sam's finger where it rested on his napkin. The too-sharp touch pricked his knuckle.

He refused to flinch.

"Though you might want to note for next time, I prefer Burgundies."

The well-trained wine expert gulped as though he'd swallowed his tongue.

No doubt, cracking open a bottle this rare warranted at least some measure of excitement. Sam had shoveled shit an entire summer for the kind of cash he'd laid out for this extravagance. And he hadn't thought twice about it. He was willing to indulge Belinda's last-ditch effort at hard-to-get.

They shared a long glance—one that proved she

knew as well as he did where they were headed. Soon. When he peered into her soft brown eyes as he buried himself slowly, gently, she would surrender enough to satisfy them both. He could afford to be gracious.

"Sir?" The sommelier provided one last chance to balk before breaking the seal.

"Uncork it." Belinda gave the man the go-ahead to proceed with his elaborate ritual, though she never dropped eye contact with Sam.

"I thought we could celebrate early." Sam cradled her hand in his, raising it to his mouth. He brushed soft kisses over her wrist until she withdrew from the caress of his lips.

"What's the occasion?" She lifted a perfectly arched brow in his direction.

"I could pretend I'm sure of the partners' acceptance of my proposal for a new investor growth fund, headed by me. I'd rather we didn't lie to each other, though." He thought about how much better it would have been if they'd waited to open the Bordeaux until they were in bed and drank it straight from the bottle...or off each other's skin.

"I'm not sure I understand." She batted her midnight lashes.

"Oh yes, you do." He toned down his grin to avoid looking like the Cheshire cat or the big bad wolf. "We've been do-si-doing around each other for too long. I'm done circling."

"Excuse me? I don't speak hick."

"I'll class it up for you, dear." He laced their fingers and trapped her hand to the table. Her sourpuss act had him turned on beyond belief. What the hell was wrong with him? "It takes two to tango, and I'm one hell of a dancer."

"Awfully cocky, Mr. Compton."

"You can say that again." He relied on the

charisma he'd inherited from JD to take the edge off his bluntness. "Determined and a shade stubborn as well."

"Ahem." The sommelier cleared his throat as he neared with the sample of wine he'd spun around a decanter to aerate.

"Do the honors, Belinda."

Her eyes glittered as she breathed deep from the open mouth of the glass. The hard tips of her nipples made faint contours in the bust of her dress. In fact, they often did when she battled with someone in the boardroom.

Sam had noticed the quirk right away. He might even have instigated an argument or two in order to savor the spitfire's reactions.

A dribble of wine flowed between her lips, nearly wringing a groan from him. Her jaw shifted as she rolled the liquid over her palate. Finally, her throat flexed. Sam's eyes dried out as he stared.

Christ.

"It'll do."

He laughed. "Damn straight."

The rest of dinner passed in a blur. Sam scarfed the extravagant meal, committing a heinous disservice to the chef. He could have eaten a bowl of Lucky Charms for all he knew. The only thing he wanted to taste was Belinda. If he could have draped her over the table and feasted on her flesh he would have done it, the other diners be damned. Even better, really.

No, no, no. No thinking of performing sexual acrobatics for elegantly dressed witnesses. No hard-ons allowed for his exhibitionist tendencies. Not if he had his heart set on Belinda, who could hardly stand the light weight of his palm on her lower back as he escorted her to his waiting car.

"I'm taking you home with me." He didn't ask as he tucked her into the bucket seat and stole a soft kiss.

She blinked.

He grinned at her rare speechlessness, then shut the door gently. Through the smoky glass he caught her tiny smirk before he attempted a dignified sprint around to the driver's side.

Sam tried to take things slow. Before he realized it he'd peeled into his penthouse apartment's reserved garage spot and assaulted Belinda in the private elevator on the ride to the top floor. Glass walls didn't deter him one bit.

Let the world watch.

He somehow shed his clothes as he carried her to his room and laid her on the king-sized bed covered in a plush Siberian goose-down duvet and Frette linens. The burn of her appreciative stare made every lousy hour in his home gym and the fresh salads he'd eaten instead of the red meat he'd grown up on worth the aggravation even if she didn't tell him she liked what she saw. He didn't need the verbalization, not when she licked her lips and trailed one finger down his abdomen toward his rigid cock.

"You're overdressed for this party, Lin." Sam traced the ruching across her tiny waist and hummed. "Gorgeous as it is, this dress has to go."

He refused to fuck her with the silk wadded around her waist. It wasn't like he was some adolescent who couldn't wait long enough to do it right. Though, he wouldn't lie. It was close.

A shiver went through her as he slid the zipper down her side, then slipped the sheath from her, swiping her understated yet outrageous nude, platform peep-toe heels from her feet. He peeked at the designer name—Louboutin—cataloging it for future gifting.

Black lingerie over pale, pale skin had his mouth watering more than the aged porterhouse that had graced his plate earlier.

32

"Fuck me." He gritted his teeth and prayed for a sliver of restraint. Belinda wasn't like other lovers he'd indulged in since leaving Columbia, and his attempts at sweet college romance, behind. This time he was playing for keeps. Scaring her away their first night together would ruin everything.

"Yes, please." She covered his balled fist and drew it to her breast.

His fingers relaxed, plumping the handful of soft flesh coated with delicate lace. A seam popped when he teased her nipple beneath the edge of the cup. Unwilling to damage the high-quality garment, he divested her of the supportive material. Her sheer panties followed a heartbeat later.

"So damn beautiful." He traced her lips with the tip of his index finger, then used the moistened digit to circle her nipple.

Long walnut hair smothered his pillow in flowing waves as she rocked her head from side to side. He wished he'd thought to have his housekeeper bring flowers, bury the bed in rose petals or set a bottle of champagne in a bucket on the nightstand.

Instead he reached into the drawer there for a condom and rolled it on before sinking over Belinda to steal a taste of the Bordeaux from her lips. She turned her head at the last second, evading his kiss. The steady pulse in her neck drew his focus. He played with the tender spot until the beat sped slightly. How could she be so calm when he feared he'd lose control and ravish her Tasmanian-devil style any second?

The glide of their bare chests had his cock eager when it settled against the soft skin at the apex of her thighs. She seemed cool as he blanketed her, infusing her with excess warmth from his overheated body.

He would have loved to make out with her, savoring their closeness, but he didn't care to break her from whatever sensual place she'd gone to with her face angled, eyes shut. Magnificent. He nibbled her collarbone and rocked their pelvises together. The head of his cock poked at her entrance, their bodies aligned and well-fitted for each other.

Sam pushed the barest bit inside her pussy, monitoring her for any sign of objection. She gave none. Damn, she was tight. And not very wet. Why wouldn't she look at him? "How're you doing, darlin'?"

"Fine." She didn't disguise her wince as well as she might have thought.

"Not good enough." He withdrew, winding a sensual trail down her neck, across her breasts, over her belly. Getting comfy, he snuggled between her thighs. They clamped around his shoulders, making him claustrophobic. He pressed his hands to the backs of her knees and spread her wide.

"Sam!" A gasp flew through her parted lips. "What are you doing?"

"I insist on making this as good for you as it will be for me," he murmured between nuzzles of her neatly trimmed fuzz. A little prickly, like her. Nice.

"What if I'd rather you hurry and finish instead?"

He laughed before he realized she didn't join in.

"What kind of losers have you slept with, Lin?" Sam dusted dozens of kisses over her mound. Her thighs quivered, then relaxed their death grip on his head. He breathed deep, hoping to catch a hint of her arousal. Like the stallions he'd seen on the farm back home, he loved the smell of his mate. All he detected was the cloying blast of her custom perfume.

Sam took his time admiring her trim body. First with his eyes, then his hands and finally his mouth.

The howl she unleashed when he latched on to her pussy scared ten years off his life. He reared back, staring up at her to gauge the problem. She must be the most sensitive woman he'd ever pleasured, and God knew there'd been plenty. "Did I hurt you?"

"Good. So good." She purred and writhed as though she'd gone from zero to sixty faster than the Ferrari 458 Italia he'd eyed at the Park Avenue showroom last week.

Sam couldn't help it. He plopped on his haunches between her legs, wrapped his arms around his stomach and cracked up. "You sound like one of my brother's cheesy pornos."

Uh oh. Not on the recommended list of things to say the first time you make love to your girlfriend and potential wife, the woman you intend to have children with. When he surrendered to sexual instinct it became more difficult to maintain his sophistication.

Belinda sputtered, "W-What did you say?"

"If you get any more tightly wound you're going to shatter. Relax." He massaged the soles of her feet, then her ankles and up her legs to her hips as he lowered himself once more.

"Why did you stop? It was *soo* good."

"B. Quit it." He couldn't keep his mouth shut as he stared. "No woman of mine is going to settle for a fake fucking orgasm. Especially not one that bad. Jesus. How low is your opinion of me? I don't need you to cheat for me in bed."

She froze.

"Seriously." He gathered her into the crook of his arm and started all over again. It wasn't a hardship to worship her body. "No pressure. Let's get to know one another like this. If it happens, it happens. If not…there's always tomorrow. And the night after. And the night after. Just let me hold you. I'll make you feel good. I promise."

For the first time, maybe ever, she really looked

at him. Deep into his eyes.

"Ah, yeah. Like that." He smiled when she closed the small gap between them and took some initiative with a fierce, if brief, kiss.

"You really are something special, Samuel." She cupped his jaw.

"Sam."

"Hmm?" She broke the contact of their lips right when he would have burrowed deeper.

Less talking, dumbass. More kissing. Still, he couldn't help himself. Couldn't stand her screaming out the wrong thing when he managed to help her explode. "My name. It's plain old Sam. Nothing fancy on my birth certificate."

"Right. How could I have forgotten?" The glimmer of the woman he sensed deep inside her aloof exterior receded beneath her boardroom-bitch exoskeleton.

Fuck.

"But you can call me anything you like." He smiled, then explored her frown. "I'll do my best to make you happy, whatever it takes."

Her pout morphed into a weak smile. "Really?"

"Yeah. Sure." He imagined her requesting him to parade around in her thong. Okay, *almost* anything, he amended to himself.

"I'm glad you feel like that." As though he'd unleashed a tiger, she pounced. She claimed his mouth and devoured his moan. Though he would have preferred to be on top, he didn't argue when she straddled him.

Belinda planted her palms on his chest and ground her pussy over his sheathed cock in a sinful figure eight that rubbed them both into a frenzy. "Getting my way turns me on. You don't mind, do you?"

Her eyes softened as she tucked her feet onto his thighs.

His hands flopped to the sides. "Hmm. A sexy, assertive woman wonders if I'm game for letting her ride me into oblivion. Do I *mind*? Not at all. Use me if that works for you."

Of course, he should have realized, she'd prefer to call the shots.

"Don't mind if I do." She lifted up, then aimed the head of his cock at her suddenly saturated opening. Her body accommodated his girth as she sank onto his shaft.

"Damn, B." He moved without thinking, cupping her hips easily in his palms. "I can't believe this is finally real. Me, you. You're so fucking hot around me."

She smacked his wrists. "Put your hands behind your head."

"Yes, ma'am." A chuckle escaped as he considered how different the night would be from his soft, romantic imaginings. He felt kind of lazy allowing her to do all the work, but what fool would complain about a stunning lady massaging his aching cock with well-coordinated squeezes of her pussy?

He stared at her world-class rack as she began to bounce in his lap. She ground onto him until her labia kissed his balls. She wriggled with rhythmic arcs of her ass that swirled her clit on his tense muscles.

"Shit, yes." He couldn't take his eyes off her.

Glorious and proud, she rode him harder and harder. A flush crept up her chest and neck as she zoned out and fixated on her pleasure for several minutes.

He couldn't say when she refocused on him and noticed his gaze.

"Would you like to suck on my breasts, Sam?"

He had to bite his tongue to keep from begging

like some pussy-whipped boy. A horrid vision of his future, spent at the end of her leash, had his dick wilting inside the woman he'd planned to build something with. Had he made a mistake?

Before he could second-guess his decision, Belinda tipped forward and smothered him with the cleavage she manufactured when she smooshed her boobs together. Ah, shit, he'd worry about long-term later. Much later.

His hips rose off the mattress, allowing him to fuck deep in counterpoint to her escalating lunges. A wet *pop* echoed off the high-ceilings of his bedroom when she rocked backward, stealing her nipple from his suckling mouth. Her fingers sought his thighs for leverage.

Sam bent his knees, planting his feet flat on the bed. He provided her with the perfect spot to grip, and she capitalized on the opportunity.

After having only his hand for company these past few months, the snug velvet of her pussy tugged him rapidly toward climax. If she needed him to last, she'd have to slow down, let him take a more scenic route. "Lin—"

"Shut up." She slapped his cheek hard enough to have him adjusting his jaw. If she were a guy, he'd have returned the blow.

Stunned, he lay silent as she convulsed on top of him, screaming out in completion. The sporadic clamping of the tight rings of her muscles on his shaft wrung an answering orgasm from him despite his confusion over the blend of their passion and the pain radiating along the side of his face.

He shot at least half a dozen long blasts inside the condom, which kept his sperm from embedding in the fertile landscape of her womb. After the peaks and valleys of their night together, he figured it was for the best. Before he could sort out how he felt about all the developments, Belinda's wheezed gasp drew his attention to her. She leaned forward, allowing his softening cock to slip from her body.

"Oh my God." She kissed the flaming handprint that had to be glowing beneath his five o'clock shadow. "I can't believe I did that."

If he were honest, he'd admit he couldn't either. He'd never allowed a woman to strike him, for fun or otherwise. Well, unless you counted the spanking he'd taken as part of his hazing for the frat house, which had jumpstarted his unflagging obsession with public sex.

Something about Belinda's confession sounded so genuine he couldn't help but gather her to his side. She trembled as he rocked her.

"It's okay, baby."

"No." Her hair brushed his pecs when she shook her head. "I hit you! I jeopardized everything. For what? A momentary high, no matter how delicious."

She shuddered in his arms.

"We all have our kinks, B." He stroked her cheek, adoring the vulnerable side she revealed to him. For once, she accepted tenderness from him, allowing him to coddle her. "I'm really thankful you trusted me enough to be honest about yours."

Maybe someday he'd tell her about his unusual desires. Though, after tonight, he couldn't imagine her allowing him to fuck her in front of other men and especially doubted she'd permit them to join in. Unless she could take the reins.

Hell, he hadn't risen to his level in business without expert negotiation skills. Compromise he could do. A smile spread across his face.

"You came so hard."

"You're telling me." He sighed.

"I'm really glad you enjoyed…that." She dropped

her forehead onto his shoulder. "I was worried."

"Is that why you've kept me at arm's length for so damn long?" He groaned. "If you'd told me what you needed—"

"Sometimes it's not easy to share. Even with someone you *care* about." She kissed the side of his neck.

He groaned.

"I mean, you haven't exactly been honest with me, have you? You like to keep your secrets too."

Sam froze. Could she know about his antics at *Ménage Amore*? It would be a relief to put everything on the table.

"I'm not asking you to divulge your proposal to me, but it would be nice to know you put as much faith in me as I have in you." Her muscles stayed relaxed against his side. She didn't pressure him.

"That?" He levered onto his elbows so he could look into her eyes. "You want to hear my pitch? Work in bed?"

"Watching you trade always makes me hot." She cupped her breast and pressed her pussy to his hip. "I respect your drive."

"I could say the same for you." If that's all it took to rev her up again, he'd be happy to oblige. "Plus, I wouldn't turn down a chance to practice. I've gone over it a million times in my mind, but you're great at fine-tuning an offer. If you don't mind—"

"Not at all. I'd love to hear it." She sat with her legs cast to the side, looking for all the world like a Grecian statue of Aphrodite.

"Great, thanks. And if I get nervous tomorrow, I'll picture this—sharing with you, naked—instead of those sharks in their thousand dollar suits." He grinned. "You're going to be my good luck charm, Belinda."

"I think I can say the same." She laced her fingers

with his. "I'm so glad I met you."

He kissed her knuckles, then launched into his speech.

Chapter Three

Sam wove between lines of stopped taxis and pedestrians jaywalking left and right. He cranked up the stereo in the Maserati and belted out the next verse of Travie McCoy's "Billionaire". Sunshine had him squinting behind his tinted D&G glasses. The only thing that could have made the morning better would have been if Belinda had still shared his bed when he woke up.

After incorporating her suggestions last night, the last shred of his uncertainty had evaporated. His idea, the delivery, his standing with the company—each aspect for this morning's meeting had been polished from nearly perfect to flawless.

Vice President Compton. It had a nice ring to it.

"Good morning, Frank." Sam beamed as he rolled down the window for the firm's lot attendant.

"Mr. Compton." His usual teasing grin was nowhere to be found. "I'm going to need you to park next to the booth this morning. We'll ride up to the office together."

"Everything all right?" Sam canted his head. They'd had a rash of break-ins a few months ago. Other than a handful of stolen laptops, nothing had been damaged. Could someone have raided the building again?

"I'm not at liberty to say, sir."

What the fuck? Was this the same man he'd snuck donuts with a few times a week? The same guy whose wife had baked him a lovely plate of cookies for Christmas last year when he'd confessed he missed Vicky's homemade treats?

Sam parked and leapt from the car, eager to find out what had Frank's tighty-whiteys in a bunch. Neither one disturbed the awkward silence in the elevator as they rode up to their suite. Frank escorted him straight to Gandle's office. Maybe the partners decided to fuck with him to see if they could throw him off his game in one final test.

Lucretia, the firm's executive assistant, announced his arrival to the partners via intercom without a hint of her usual smile, so he saved the chit-chat and recounted the introductory lines of his pitch instead. When the door buzzed open, he strode past Frank, who ushered him inside. All three partners—Smith, Winfield and Gandle—faced him.

"Compton."

"Morning, Jack." It'd been years since he addressed the man as Mr. Smith. "I'm glad we're getting an early start today. I'm excited to share my proposition for a revolutionary new capital growth fund."

"You mean one heavily focused on emerging markets, yet risk-reduced through the offsetting beta of commodities like oil and diamond futures?"

Sam sputtered as months of research was laid on the line like common knowledge. "How? Have you been spying on my files?"

"Hardly." Winfield edged closer. The weight of

Frank's not-so-friendly hand pinned Sam to his seat. "Belinda suspected you'd try to claim her strategies. She came to us this morning and told us everything."

"Wait. What?" Sam shook his head, trying to decipher what he'd just been accused of by the man he'd respected for years. "She told you about last night?"

"Then you're not denying it?" Gandle scrubbed his hand over his face. "We'd hoped there was some other explanation."

"I mean, I know it's not the brightest idea. Sure. We've been seeing each other outside of the office for a few months now."

"Dating? Is that what you're calling it?" Winfield sneered at him.

"What else?"

"Belinda labeled it harassment. You pressuring her for concepts. Trying to get ahead and threatening her." Smith stood now, slamming his hands on the desk. "We won't tolerate our employees being treated that way."

"What about false accusations?" Sam would have paced the room but Frank kept him in his seat. "You apparently have no problem with those. That bitch—"

"That's enough." Gandle cut him off. "I think it's best if you leave the premises now. If you have something more to say, you can do it through your lawyer. We've all made mistakes, son."

"I'm not your child," Sam roared. "Don't treat me like one."

"You're acting it now." Smith sighed. "We're going easy on you, Sam. You've made significant contributions to this firm and your work ethic has never been questioned before. I don't care to think how many others you may have *borrowed* from. Still, go quiet and we won't put cause of discharge on your record. We have a severance package drafted—"

"Fuck you." He glared at Frank. "Take your hand off me. I'm leaving."

He burst into the lobby. Belinda tottered past, mincing her steps. She wrestled with a tri-fold board wallpapered in charts and graphs she must have raced to assemble after picking his brain last night. She looked haggard enough to validate his theory, though to the partners... Well, it played right into her story, didn't it?

Sam growled at her before he could stop the primal sound from erupting from his chest.

"Stay the hell away from her." Winfield looked as though he might explode.

"She told us how she had to fight you off. You may have tried to hide the evidence, but I can still see the imprint of her fingers on your cheek, exactly where she told us she slapped you." Smith shook his head. "We can't condone that kind of behavior from an executive in the firm."

Sam's heart dropped all the way to the basement, thirty-five floors below his body. "Excuse me?"

"Belinda has refused to press charges despite my encouragement." Gandle looked as though he'd like to spit on Sam.

"Because she can't prove something that never happened." A glimmer of doubt seeded in Sam's mind. She was convincing and would stop at nothing to come out on top. He saw that now. People might give her the benefit of the doubt in a he-said-she-said case.

"Even if I believed you"—Winfield grimaced—"there's no chance we'll allow you to stay employed. The negligence suits we'd subject ourselves to... We can't afford that kind of publicity. And we certainly won't risk her leaving. Not after the plan she proposed this morning."

"*My* plan."

"Smith, Winfield and Gandle's now." Gandle strode toward his desk. "Get him out of here, Frank."

Sam slouched in his car, his hands completely numb. He'd parked at the curb on some random side street, since he didn't have a clue where to drive to, and watched oblivious New Yorkers stream past.

For four hours.

The lunch crowd had come and gone. And still he lingered.

What he really needed was his twin. But Sawyer had left on an eight-week assignment at sea and couldn't be reached.

In that moment he realized how alone he truly was. Sure he had friends—people he'd met along the path to the corner office at Smith, Winfield and Gandle. The motherfucking, piece of shit workspace that cold fish, cock-not-sucking Vice President Belinda McJudas would settle her thousand dollar high-heels in as she hunkered down to run his growth fund.

None of his acquaintances could replace his brothers.

He stopped his fist a fraction of an inch from slamming into the dashboard. No point in hurting his baby. For some reason, Seth's face popped into the midnight behind Sam's scrunched lids. "Slow it down there. Take a deep breath. Tell me what's got you so pissed off and we'll fix it."

The same speech his brother had given when he'd spotted Sam in the barn, beating the shit out of a bag of feed one afternoon. He'd been in tenth grade. Roger Latner had somehow copied Sam's American-history essay and taken credit for it after pretending to end their long-standing feud and be study buddies.

What the fuck? Did he have sucker tattooed

somewhere in the mural of Compass Ranch?

He banged his head on the leather steering wheel, then drew his phone from his suit pocket. Suddenly his clothes suffocated him. He dialed Seth and yanked at the knot on his tie.

The line seemed to connect, but Seth didn't speak immediately.

Sam stared at the screen of the device. It indicated the line was open. Maybe Seth didn't have a great signal at home. If he'd joined his brother, maybe none of this would have happened. With his presentation approaching, he hadn't considered more than half a second. He'd declined. For what?

Before he could test the line, a familiar though ragged voice zapped across the country when he needed it most. "Hey, bro."

"Hey, Seth." Both of them sounded as though they'd eaten a cheese grater for breakfast.

In addition to his anger, misery, frustration and outrage, a knife of fear cut into Sam. Something wasn't right. The world was going crazy.

"What's wrong?" Seth whispered.

Shit, shit, shit. That kind of pain hadn't mangled his brother's voice since the day after Silas left Compass Ranch. Change of plans. If Sam's family needed him, he would be there. They came first. Always had, always would. No one else cared for him like they did. No one else warranted his loyalty.

"Who says something's wrong?" Sam locked the sickness in his gut in a deep pit for examination later. Focusing on Seth counteracted some of the blinding agony. He gave it one last-ditch effort in case the bomb that had annihilated his life had made him overdramatic. "Where are you? You sound…fucked up. I thought poker night wasn't 'til Wednesday. Are you hungover?"

"No. It's not… Look, I c-can't think right now. Focus on the point. You called me." Seth had never lost it like this. Calm, easygoing, patient—Seth didn't shake easily. Whatever had his brother so rattled had to be a travesty. "Pardon me for saying so, but you don't sound like you're skipping through daisies yourself."

In that moment, nothing mattered but standing by his brother, no matter what he needed. Without hesitation, Sam announced, "I'm coming home."

Not like I have a job to worry about anymore.

A shaky *oomph* puffed over the phone as though Seth had collapsed. "Thank God."

"What the hell?" Sam's tenuous hold on sanity slipped a little. This had to be bad. What if he couldn't handle another ounce of despair despite his good intentions? "I tell you my cock ruined seven years of hard work for one moronic, not-even-that-great fuck and you say *thank God?*"

"Yeah." A wet gulp followed as his brother swallowed hard. "It's JD."

His tone said it all.

"What the fuck? Seth! Don't stop now. Jesus. What's going on back there?"

Seth cleared his throat. "JD has pancreatic cancer, Sam. He's dying."

Dying? JD couldn't possibly be sick. He was the strongest man on the planet—a badass cowboy. And young. Youngish. Actually, now that Sam thought about it, he had twenty years on Vicky. That must put him at… Damn, could that be? Close to seventy?

Somehow JD seemed ageless, constant, permanent.

"Christ," Sam choked. In one morning his personal universe had undergone a big bang. The fabric of his existence unraveled thread by thread, faster than he could stop it. "I'll be home tonight."

"When does your flight get in? I'll pick you up." Seth assumed he'd already had something scheduled

Instead of burdening his brother with unnecessary details, Sam would make it work. Cost was no object. He did some quick calculations in his mind and guesstimated. "Six hours from now. Don't worry. I'll find my own way. You have more to worry about than me."

"Don't be a dumbass. I'll always be there for you. We'll talk on the ride in. I could use an ear myself, okay?"

Heat blasted Sam's cheeks as he braced himself for recounting the sordid details of his disgraceful exit from his dream job. Not exactly the triumphant news he'd hoped to call home with. *Shit.* And on top of that, Seth needed someone to have his back. What more could there be than the horrific news he'd shared?

Had Sam really heard his brother right? JD. Dying?

Another shot of dread-laced adrenaline spiked his heart rate. He rubbed the ache in his stomach.

"Yeah. Okay," Sam mumbled when the silence lingered. "Pancreatic cancer. There's no hope, is there?"

"Not for JD."

Oh God. If Seth was there, if he'd heard the news, then Silas must already know but... "Sawyer."

Their youngest brother had idolized JD growing up. Though they'd all been close, the connection was strongest between those two. Maybe JD had seen shades of himself in Sawyer's Dom tendencies even when they were kids.

"He has no clue. Fuck. I'm sitting here outside the doctor's office. Mom doesn't even know yet."

Sam wrestled sobs, which threatened to choke him, into a giant sigh. He would have flown to San

Francisco to tell Sawyer in person except... "He's out at sea. Got that special assignment he's been gunning for. He left yesterday."

"How long will he be away?"

"About two months." Sam had been so caught up in his project he hadn't paid enough attention. Eight weeks, he'd guess. What kind of asshole had he been that he hadn't really listened one hundred percent? A self-absorbed asshole, that's what kind. "When he gets back, he has two week's leave at which point he told me he was turning off his phone and fucking himself into oblivion."

Seth chuckled softly. "Has he decided about re-upping yet?"

"No. I think he was gonna figure out his future while he's at sea."

Seth considered that. "Maybe we should let him make that decision before we tell him about JD."

"Shit," Sam muttered. Did they have that kind of time? "He'll kill us."

"Like you said, he's not going to be able to come home for at least two months. Let him have this time to get his shit together. If things take a turn for the worst, then we'll get him home sooner. Somehow."

"Okay. So you haven't told Mom?"

Seth sighed wearily. "No."

Oh fuck. Vicky. It would be harder to bear for her than JD. The two had always been inseparable. He could help them be strong. They were better together. "I want to be there when you do."

Seth breathed deep several times in a row. "Okay."

"So I'll see you at the airport?" He couldn't wait to be there. With Seth. If he could drive several hundred miles an hour, he'd tear out of this godforsaken city and haul ass directly to Wyoming.

"Yeah."

"I'll text you the flight info." Staying professional would help him brazen through this. But some part of him, the fraction that might still be ten years old, didn't understand how to do that. "Seth?"

"Yeah?"

"We're gonna get through this, right?" Sam's voice cracked and he didn't pretend otherwise.

It reminded him of the time he'd tumbled out of the hayloft. Pain had raced up his leg, then his spine. Seth had carried him to the truck while Sawyer ran to get their folks. Sam had only been ten at the time, and he'd looked at Seth as his savior, asking him if his leg would be okay, if he'd be crippled or walk with a limp.

These days it was Silas fighting that battle, his injuries far worse than Sam's simple fracture. Good thing they had grown stronger. They'd have to be to survive a wound deeper and more painful than all the individual injuries they'd suffered combined.

Seth said now what he'd said then. "We're gonna get through this just fine."

Sam hung up the phone, praying his brother's words were true.

Chapter Four

Mountains glowed with late afternoon sunshine, welcoming Sam home. Blue-black streams snaked through canyons from snow-capped heights. They bisected golden prairies and fed glittering lakes nestled among lush green grass. As vividly as if it had been yesterday, he remembered this scenery in reverse—cattle shrinking into tiny specks in the vast landscape as he jetted off to a cosmopolitan paradise.

One that had become his own personal hell.

He'd had plenty of time to reflect on Belinda, his career and JD on the trip across the country. Funny how what had seemed like an apocalypse this morning seemed almost inconsequential when faced with the fleetingness of life. The more he considered the future he'd begged for, then slaved over, the more he wondered why he'd sacrificed so much for The Man.

It had never been about money. Sure, that part was nice. He had expensive tastes and loved to indulge in fancy toys. But none of them had ever made him as happy as achieving his independence. A young kid from a rural, work-to-the-bone background could transform into someone powerful, smart and important.

At least, he'd been determined to make that leap.

Too bad he'd have had all those things anyway if he'd stayed home.

It hadn't seemed the same to him. He'd itched to earn it, not inherit it, and he supposed he'd shown the only person who mattered—himself—that it was possible. He'd traveled the world both as a foreign exchange student in London and during a three-month triumphant stint after he'd graduated with honors from Columbia. He'd studied with top talent in his field, experienced cultural diversification and engaged in sexual adventures he never could have found on Compass Ranch.

So he was confident down to his marrow. No other place would live up to this one.

No matter what lay in front of them, he didn't intend to leave home again unless it was on vacation. With technology, he could trade from here as well as he could from The Street. Surrounded by people with integrity and hearts brimming with generous love, he couldn't ask for more.

If only they needed him, too.

Colby, Si and Seth could help with the physical shit he'd never mastered while he focused on managing the business side of JD's empire. He prepared to share his plan with Seth as diligently as he had crafted his fund pitch.

Sinking steadily on the escalator, he had an eagle-eye view of the crowd milling around the luggage carousel. When he caught sight of Seth, slumped with his hands jammed in the pockets of ripped Levi's, Sam switched gears. The guy couldn't have looked more miserable if he were the poster child for some bizarre disease that rotted your cock off.

Middle of the airport or not, Sam didn't give a fuck. He strode to Seth and yanked him into a fierce, one-armed hug. Damn, he'd always been a tough son of a bitch, but years of labor had filled him out. After relying on pictures and conference calls, Sam admitted Seth was even more impressive in person.

"Whatever it is, we'll figure it out." He promised his brother.

"Not whatever." Seth groaned. "Whoever."

"A woman. It figures." Sam squeezed Seth harder. He could relate. "Tell me about it. Did she fuck around on you?"

"Jody?" He shook his head. "No, she screwed around *with* me."

"What?" Sam couldn't have heard that right. "You slept with someone else's girlfriend?"

"Fiancée actually."

"Wow." Sam tilted his head. He'd swear Seth wasn't joking. Mr. Squeaky Clean would have to go temporarily insane with lust, or love, to do something like that. "Uh, maybe you'd better fill me in."

It took the entire ride home to explain Seth's relationship woes. Sam didn't mind relegating his drama to the backburner. It all seemed like a crazy dream in any case. It wasn't as if talking things through would change the end result for him.

Seth still had a chance.

By the time they passed the ranch's property line, Sam thought he might have gotten off lucky. At least he hadn't lost his heart to Belinda. Only his pride.

"She'll come around, Seth." Sam caught the hopelessness in his brother's eyes. "And if she doesn't, she deserves to marry that other guy."

"No, Jody deserves the best." Seth accelerated despite the bumps in the gravel-covered grooves that formed the long driveway. "I may not be perfect, but I would love her with everything I have. Shit, Sam, I've done that for years already. I wish you could meet her."

"Meet her? Bro, I've already seen her naked." Sam ducked when Seth took a swipe at him.

At least Seth laughed. "Sexy as hell, isn't she?"

"Not too shabby." Sam smiled as his brother parked the truck.

"And, fuck, we should have decided what the plan of attack is here." Seth glanced at him from the corner of his eye. "You have to be ready. When you see JD. Well, it's been a while, right?"

"Almost three years." Sam stared out the window at every rock and tree he knew by heart.

"It's okay, Sam." Seth angled toward him, buying them a little more time. "We each had to follow our own path. They know that. They're okay with it. At least you didn't pull a Silas and stay gone an entire decade. But…try to act like JD's the same, okay?"

"That bad?" A ball of unease slid through his guts.

"I'm surprised no one here called it out sooner." He sighed. "I think he might have been fighting this for a while by himself. You know how he is. And to tell the truth, he's older and it's starting to show. Kind of freaked me out at first. So different from the guy I remember. But he's the same JD inside."

"Stubborn? Determined? Fair? Hardworking?"

"Yeah. Don't forget kickass. If you rate it, he'll take you down, then help you find your feet again." Seth groaned. "He cornered me this morning about going after Jody."

"You told him?" Sam wondered what their father had thought of Seth kidnapping another rancher's daughter and making love to her regardless of her sham engagement. "Brave."

"Fuck no, not all the details. Didn't have to anyway. I think he might have called Thomas." His brother smacked his head on the window. "God help me if her dad teams up with JD."

"I've got your back, Seth." Sam slapped his brother's thigh, waking him out of his trance. "No matter what. At least I'll help you with a head start when the dude busts through the front door with a shotgun."

"Gee, thanks. Asshole." Seth grinned as he climbed out.

Sam dropped from the oversized pickup. Dust in the yard puffed beneath the soles of his Cole Haan wingtips and clung to his black trousers. His urban uniform would have to go. Jeans and boots, he must have packed some cowboy essentials, right?

He couldn't for the life of him remember what he'd stuffed in his Samsonite carry-on.

With one hand on the door of the truck, he glanced up at the scene he'd borne on his skin for close to a decade. It'd resided in his heart far longer. Live and in person, not flipped in the mirror after a shower, it took him a second to reorient himself.

The modern pin-up standing dead center, outside the barn door, was a nice addition. Petite, blond—except for a few crazy yet stylish lavender highlights—she sported fashionable, thick-framed glasses that would make her look like an unassuming nerd if every instinct didn't scream better. A trendy denim skirt, cowgirl boots and a ruffled silk blouse rounded out her simply sexy ensemble.

Their eyes met and locked.

"Jesus, Sam." Seth's low growl wouldn't travel to the woman making Sam's cock stir despite the long, hard winter he'd promised the tool for being tricked by fancy ass. "Take a fucking picture, why don't you?"

"Who is she?" He grimaced, then spun toward the main house. "Never mind. Don't answer that."

Seth laughed. "Cindi could be just what you need

to forget whatever tucked your tail between your legs. I'd offer to return the ear you lent me tonight, but you might be better off in her oh-so-capable hands. She's sweet as can be, and I've heard she's pretty wild. Careful though, JD has sort of adopted her. Sick or not, he'll crush you if you hurt her."

"No one's getting hurt. Fuck. No one's getting anything." Sam couldn't believe they were having this conversation. "In fact, I think I might try a strictly no-sex diet for a while."

"You and me both." Seth scrubbed his face.

When he opened his eyes again, Sam thought he might have seen the sheen of tears there. *Holy fuck.* "Don't worry, Seth. I'm sure there's some other explanation for your girl. She read your note. She'll come around. Knowing you, you probably picked the most stubborn filly in the lot. Serves you right, fucker."

His goading had exactly the intended effect. Seth laughed as he grappled with Sam, putting him in a headlock long enough to attempt the mother of all noogies.

"Oh, ho. I see you've been working out. You're hiding some power in that scrawny little frame." Seth shook his head as they declared a truce.

Only next to his brothers would he be considered weak. Was it any wonder he'd learned to show off his physical prowess to admiring crowds? They sauntered up to the house with Seth's arm flung across his back.

Sam peeked over his shoulder. The woman—Seth had called her Cindi—leaned against the barn with one foot on the wall, her knee bent. She grinned in their direction.

Damn.

He tripped on the first of the porch steps and whipped around to avoid a full-out face plant. Great first impression.

Seth's grip steadied him.

"Thanks."

"I'll always be right here." Seth paused with one hand on the door to the kitchen.

"Same goes, bro."

"You ready?"

"Let's do it." Sam nodded. They rushed inside like cops on a raid.

From behind Seth's broad shoulders, Sam first caught sight of Silas and Colby sandwiching Lucy on one side of the dining room table. Lucy's eyes grew wide as she stared in his direction. She might have jumped up to greet him if Silas hadn't laid a restraining hand on her forearm. Though she quieted instantly, the warmth in her smile packed as big of a punch as a bear hug. It smothered him with her welcome.

"The chicken will be done in a minute." Vicky's announcement drifted closer. "Why don't you kids start with some salad while you're waiting? Oh, Seth. They said you were running errands. Wash up and join—"

Seth took a giant step to the side.

Lettuce flew in every direction. A carrot bounced off the lamp hanging over the table, setting it to swinging in a soft arc. Colby snatched the sage ceramic bowl before it smashed on the plank flooring.

"Hi." Sam tried to smile. It probably came out more like a weird pout. Overwhelming emotions, so intense they defied description or even identification, paralyzed him. For the first time in his life, Sam saw his sharp, sassy mother without a single thing to say. She stood with her mouth open, sputtering.

Then she put one hand over her heart and wobbled.

He rushed forward, brushing Seth aside, and scooped her into his arms.

"Sam." She stroked his cheek. "Is it really you?"

"Yeah, Ma." He hugged her so tight she squeaked. "It's me."

"But it's not my birthday or Mother's Day or Christmas... What are you doing here?"

Silas barked a laugh no one else echoed.

"Oh no." Lids more wrinkled than he remembered hid her eyes.

"Do you feel okay?" Sam led her to a chair at the table. He'd never seen her react like this. The subtle indications of her shock seemed as wild as hysterics from his steadfast mother. "Sorry, I shouldn't have surprised you like that. I wasn't thinking."

"No, no. It's okay. Better than." She kept her hand in constant contact with him, patting his arm and squeezing his knee as he settled beside her. "God, how I've missed you."

"Same here." He thanked his brothers for not ridiculing the hitch in his admission.

"It's just that—"

JD chose then to amble into the room. Good thing Sam already sat. His father looked as though he'd aged ten years in the three since Sam had seen him last. He seemed to have shrunk. Where before his jeans would have stretched tight over powerful muscles, they hung baggy on his frame. His tan had faded to yellowish and his salt and pepper hair had transitioned to completely silver.

"Welcome home, son."

"JD." He couldn't manage more than that. And before he could figure out what to say, Vicky had torn from his grasp and launched herself across the room.

"How dare you keep secrets from me?" She shocked the shit out of them all by laying her palms flat on her husband's chest and shoving.

JD didn't budge a fraction of an inch.

"I didn't know Sam was coming." He shook his

head as he stared at Vicky. Her burst of energy caved easily to his soothing arms as he tucked his petite wife against his side. They fit together so perfectly it was hard to imagine them apart.

"JD Compton, that is *not* what I meant and you damn well know it." Her fingers balled. She crumpled his loose shirt in her fists. "Just tell me already. I can't stand you all staring at me like this. It's bad. Real bad. Don't you think I've noticed? You're slower to climb out of bed in the morning. All that tossing and turning at night. The endless coughing you're trying to hide. Silas and Seth are home. Now Sam. Say it, JD. Please. Just say it. I can't keep ignoring this anymore and pretending everything is peachy. Damn you. *Say. It.*"

JD looked to the ceiling, took a giant breath, then gripped his wife's shoulders in his gnarled fingers. He stared straight into her eyes and put it simple. "I'm dying. Ain't got much time left. I'm so sorry for leaving you. You know I'd never do it if I had a choice."

No tears streamed down her face.

No angry curses burst from her lips.

No bitterness marred her innate grace.

Instead, she nodded and focused on the facts. "Were you at Dr. Cahill's this morning? Is that where you boys went?"

"Yes. They wouldn't shut the hell up about it." JD rolled his eyes. "I already told them what the tests would show. Now it's for sure."

"Is there any point in a second opinion? Any treatments to try? What exactly are we talking about here?" Her shoulders spread as she braced herself.

Sam had never met anyone as brave as his mom.

"It's stage three pancreatic cancer, babe." JD nuzzled her hair. "I'm sorry. *So* damn sorry. I'd do anything I could to stay with you and the boys. Anything. I've been fighting as hard as I can."

"You always have." She kissed his cheek extra softly.

Sam thought his chest might shatter. He'd trade every penny he'd earned to buy them more time together—days, hours, minutes or even seconds. Some things were priceless.

"I'm tired, V." JD rested his forehead against his wife's. As if a huge burden had been lifted from his shoulders, he sagged. Colby reached him first as Silas tried to shift his bad leg and stand.

Lucy restrained the eldest Compass Brother with a feather-light touch of her fingertips on Si's scarred arm. They embraced while JD allowed the ranch's foreman to usher him and Vicky to the table.

Colby spun toward the kitchen peninsula and filled a glass full of cold well water. Then he snagged a bottle of whiskey too. He held both out to Vicky.

She smiled at him. "Thank you, honey."

A clink followed the cap bouncing on the table. She strangled the neck of the Johnnie Walker Black Label and glugged several fingers worth of liquor straight from the bottle.

Silas stared at the rich tawny liquid.

Their mom didn't offer it to him. Instead, she calmly replaced the top, then set it on the floor, out of sight. She allowed herself one tiny sniffle. "For so long I've prayed to have my sons back home. More than one at a time. For longer than a day or two. And now that you're here, it isn't what I imagined. I'm afraid, well... It's silly, right? Careful what you wish for and all."

"Don't talk crazy." JD rubbed her lower back. "This isn't anyone's fault. It's life. It's how things work. Hell, we always knew it'd probably come to this. The only thing I hated about being older than you. I never wanted to leave you alone."

Vicky buried her face in JD's blue and black

plaid work-shirt. "I love you. So much. Don't worry about me. As long as the ranch is standing, I'll never be lonely. We've built something together that will outlast us all. This place. Our family. Our sons."

"Hardheaded. Every last one." JD stared at each person around the table in turn. "I went to the doctor for you today. Now hear this. No more tests. No more poking, prodding or wasting what time I've got to spend on earth. You have something to call it now. The end result is the same."

Lucy piped up. The nurse in her refused to be cowed by her father-in-law's mandate. "There are plenty of things we can do to improve your quality of life in the coming months."

"I don't think I have that long left in me." JD shrugged. "But if it won't keep me from doing what I need to around here, training these kids to run the place, I'll listen to what you tell me. You're the expert, okay?"

She nodded.

"Sometime tomorrow I'd like you to lay it on the line for me. How's it going to go down? I need to be prepared." He didn't flinch from the truth.

"Oh God." Lucy's mascara ran along with the trails of her tears. "I love you, JD. I won't lie. This is going to be…brutal."

Both Silas and Colby edged closer, cradling her between them.

"Think of me like one of the horses. Your pa was one hell of a vet. He destroyed animals he loved a hundred times over. You're strong like him. Separate your job from the rest. We'll do just fine. And if it's too much, that's okay too, girly. There are other—"

"Never. No one else will care for you. The hardest part for you won't be the pain or fear of the unknown. I know you, JD. It'll be the loss of dignity that challenges you most. No one else will see it. I swear. We'll deal with this in the family." Lucy reached across the table for his hand when he didn't respond. "All of us, together."

"Sawyer?" Vicky looked to Sam.

"He doesn't know. His assignment started yesterday. It'll be eight weeks before he's done." He squinted toward JD. Did they have that kind of time? "I think we should have the Coast Guard airlift him out."

"Absolutely not." The head of Compass Ranch rapped his knuckles on the table as he laid down the law. "That boy's been working toward this for a long time."

"It's not your choice, JD." Sam tried again. Sawyer had a right to know. He should be here. He would opt to come home.

What if Sawyer never had a chance to say goodbye? Would he ever forgive them? It had seemed unfathomable this morning, but the reality stared Sam in the face now. It was a definite possibility.

"Quit sizing me up. I'm not going to keel over. Eight weeks you say?" JD gritted his teeth. "I've got that in me yet. I'll fight for every one of those damn days. Mark my words. Give him a chance to do his thing. I'll still be here when he's done."

Sam knew if anyone could defy nature, it'd be his dad. At least for a little while. He never did anything half-assed and his will shone through the pain in his eyes. Besides, if things deteriorated, Sam could always make the call then.

"Somebody better grab that chicken." JD motioned with his chin. "Smells like it might be burning."

They all let Sam pretend he hopped to because he was hungry. He dried his tears on the kitchen towel, which draped over the handle of the oven door, before he removed the roasting pan. Savory steam blasted him.

Instead of making his mouth water, it turned his stomach. Even his mom's awesome secret recipe couldn't stir his appetite.

Dinner sat in his gut like a brick when Vicky rose. "Would you kids mind dish duty?"

"Of course not," Colby answered first, and they all concurred.

She bit her lip as she stroked Sam's hair.

"I'm not going anywhere," he promised. "We can catch up in the morning, Ma."

"It's a date. You, me and blueberry waffles. Your room is all ready for you."

"But how?" He frowned.

"She always keeps it like that." JD clapped Sam on the shoulder hard enough to draw a grunt from him, then trundled off toward his and Vicky's bedroom.

The couple leaned against each other, taking it slow but steady. Murmurs trailed behind them, too soft to decipher. The last thing Sam saw as they rounded the corner was their fingers.

Laced together.

Chapter Five

Cindi shook her head as Seth helped his brother up the stairs. She didn't have to be introduced to recognize the man who'd ridden in with the southern charmer. Another one of the infamous Compass Brothers had returned.

Magnets from the four corners of the country, not to mention several places around the world, pinned pictures of Vicky's heartbreakers to the refrigerator in the main house. Even without the recent headshot of one of New York's top traders, she'd have had no trouble identifying JD's offspring.

Sam had inherited his father's build and the easy flow of his movements. Something about him called to her even more than the other potent Compton men. Maybe it'd been his sophisticated style, his understated yet quality clothing or his classic haircut, which highlighted his handsomeness more than his ruggedness.

In person, he blew away the photo she'd drooled over when putting up leftovers. *Damn.*

"Careful, sweetie." Jake approached from where he'd been tinkering with a piece of equipment. He wiped the grease off his hands onto his jeans before trailing his index finger down her neck. "You're looking like you might swallow that talented tongue of yours."

"Jealous?" She lifted a brow.

"Maybe." He shrugged. "Can't imagine a Compass Brother sharing his girl. That'd be a mighty big problem. For both of us I'd reckon."

"You do realize Silas has sex with both Colby and Lucy, right?" She adored the blush that enhanced his deep tan.

"That's different." He shook his head. "You know what I'm talking about. Or if you've forgotten, maybe I could show you. Pretty sure Duke, Johnny and Levi are finishing up inside. We'll make you forget you ever saw that kid. Pussy city-slickers like him don't have anything on real men."

"Not tonight, Jake." For the first time, the idea of a romp in the hay with them didn't appeal. Usually an invitation to be embraced by their group inspired a shiver. Not today. "And don't talk like that, okay? It doesn't improve my opinion of you."

"Really, Cin?" He retreated a step or two as though she were one of her beloved barn cats, hissing and slashing at him with sharp claws. "Is that how it is? I always thought you didn't care about a man's standing as much as his open arms. We've made you part of our family, given you what you needed. The second you see some rich prick you're going to throw us over? Hell, you've never even talked to the guy."

"Don't you think you're getting ahead of yourself?" She chuckled. "All I'm doing is standing here, enjoying the evening air and the scenery."

"I've seen that look before." Jake came closer. He crowded her against the wall, but she didn't flinch. He'd never hurt her.

When he bent his head and stole a kiss, she added

enough heat to the brief glide of her lips to reassure him.

"I like it better when it's aimed at me," he whispered in her ear. "Have your fun. I'll be ready to pick up the pieces."

"What do you have against Sam?" She tilted her head as she studied the tightness in Jake's jaw. He was one of the most relaxed, easygoing cowboys she'd ever met.

"It's hard to respect a kid who doesn't appreciate his good fortune." Jake shook his head. "I'd have killed for the kind of folks he has, the support he threw in the garbage. All of the Compass Brothers."

"Didn't they leave right after high school?" That's what ranch rumor had to say about it, anyway.

"Yeah. All of them lit out of here like their asses were on fire, the moment they turned eighteen. Silas… Of all of them, I get how that situation could fuck with your head. Maybe." He kicked at a rock. "The rest, well, I don't fucking understand."

"You can't judge what they did as teenagers, Jake." She snagged his hand and squeezed. "You're older. We both know how important these kinds of connections are. They were lucky. They didn't have a clue what it's like to be totally alone, like us. Never will probably."

"I hope you're right." The cheerful mask he typically wore drooped a fraction, and Cindi couldn't resist their bond. Jake had provided a safe haven for her when she needed it. Tonight seemed like a bad night for him. "Wouldn't wish that on anybody."

She leaned toward the open door, tugging on him gently. "Your offer still stand?"

"Why?" He peered from beneath the brim of his dark, dusty hat.

"I think I changed my mind." She walked

backward, drawing him into the barn.

"I ain't interested in a pity fuck, Cin."

"Shut up already, cowboy." She cut her criticism with a soft smile. "I have better uses for your mouth."

"Hell." He groaned when she slipped her fingers into his waistband and led him toward the three men leaning against an empty stall, shooting the shit.

Several hours later, Cindi sat behind her desk in the barn. A soft lamp illuminated the paperwork she'd been distracted from earlier. Okay, so maybe she really needed an excuse to avoid letting Jake or any of the other guys drive her to the cute cottage she'd claimed. It sat on top of a hill blanketed in wildflowers, which overlooked a pond on the ranch's property. JD had told her it'd belonged to one of his aunts back in the day.

When she'd first seen it, she doubted it would ever be habitable again.

Jake, Colby, Duke, Johnny, Levi and no less than a dozen other cowboys had lent their strong backs to help her renovate the place. JD had allowed her to manage the ranch's office in exchange for room and board. Their community had built her sanctuary, infusing it with their generosity and hospitality. To protect her standing, she hadn't allowed a single visitor since she'd moved in about two years ago. Except for Vicky, who would stop by for a cup of tea on occasion, or JD. But she didn't have any secrets from them.

Most of the time, the hands knew better than to beg to stay the night. Jake had grown a little clingy lately. She refused to give him false hope. She would never choose only him. Monogamy didn't suit her, and she wasn't the kind of woman who'd cheat on her man.

Besides, she couldn't risk anyone spying on her retreat if she had any hope of protecting the life she'd built here. Sacrificing her unofficial family was something she wasn't willing to do.

Twenty minutes, tops, would guarantee her lovers had drifted to the bunkhouse in a sated daze to hit the hay and she would stroll in the moonlight along the path etched into her soul. Relaxed, her body humming, assured of her place in the Compass Ranch universe, she couldn't wait to snuggle into the mountain of pillows on her bed and drift off with the chirping of the frogs in her pond for a lullaby.

She stifled a yawn.

A rustle from the main area of the barn had her dropping her head into her hands. She had hoped their physical sharing would be enough. Putting Jake in his place wouldn't be pretty. Or easy. She couldn't explain the difference between what she needed and what he had hinted he would like to try.

Shit. If things turned ugly she might have to take drastic measures.

Moving on from Compass Ranch could kill her.

Better to cut it off at the head. She hooked her fingers through the loop on her Coach wristlet, then strode from the space she'd carved from the working barn. She looked left, then right, up and down the aisle of stalls. Jake was nowhere to be seen. Still, the scuff she'd heard had sounded more like boots than the clomp of a restless horse or even the scurry of a barn mouse.

"Hello?" she called softly, goose bumps rising on her arm.

She'd never had one moment of fear in this place despite countless long nights organizing the books. JD had done his best before she'd come onboard. Still, there'd been a ton of room for improvement. The darkness had never seemed so quiet. Too still.

Someone was out there.

Someone was watching.

"If you don't show yourself I'll scream my fucking head off. Seth and Sam Compton are in the main house tonight. They'll probably land a few good shots before JD makes you wish you were never born."

"Uh, actually." A smooth, low voice stroked over her more intimately than the caresses she'd shared with Jake not long ago. "Sam Compton is in the barn. He didn't realize anyone else was still awake. And then once he figured it out, he didn't want to frighten you, seeing as you've never been formally introduced."

Cindi sucked in a breath when he emerged from the shadows carrying one of Tweety's kittens. Though the litter had grown like weeds this last week, the furball looked like a speck of fuzz cupped in Sam's broad, callous-free fingers.

"A pleasure to meet you." He tipped his hand until the kitten sank her claws in and stuck like Velcro to his tight, navy blue T-shirt. It wasn't a ratty one with some tractor brand plastered across it, but a high-quality designer variety that hugged his defined pecs.

He extended his palm in her direction.

She met him halfway.

"Likewise. I'm Cindi Middleton." Their gazes collided as he engulfed her fingers with his gentle squeeze. Pale green irises mesmerized her.

A plaintive mewl broke the moment. Cindi scooped Peaches from Sam's chest before the kitten did damage. Her knuckles brushed Sam's warmth. The languor permeating her bones didn't prevent her from snapping to attention at the instant current that arced between them. Before she realized what she intended, she'd rubbed her free hand over the tiny pinpricks in the soft fabric, erasing the disturbances in the weave.

"Hmm." Sam purred louder than the kitten.

Her stare whipped to his. She took a giant step back. "Sorry. Wasn't thinking."

"Damn, me either." He shook his head, then massaged his temples. "It's been an insane day. Pretty much the worst of my life if I'm honest. I came here for some space to think. I'd better go."

"No, wait!" Cindi didn't mean to shout. She blushed. "I was heading home. I didn't mean to intrude. Stay. It is *your* place after all."

"Is it?" He tilted his head, glancing toward her refuge. "Seems like you have more of a claim staked than me."

She bit her lip. Dangerous territory with a brooding man.

The late hour, stress and a lack of sleep blurred their judgment.

Still, she couldn't ignore the desolation in his tone. "I've only been squatting here. Compass Ranch is in your blood. Whether you were gone a minute or fifty years it wouldn't matter. Hell, not a day goes by I don't hear about the antics of those crazy Compass Brothers. Your mark is all over this place. Forever."

"None of those stories are true, I assure you." He smiled for the first time. The white, even span of his teeth brightened his entire face. The dark stain of his five o'clock shadow seemed scandalous by comparison.

She swallowed hard. "Not even the good ones?"

"Hard to believe there are many of those. Trouble has a way of finding four wild boys."

"Well, Levi told me about the time Snake's sister went into labor. Rumor has it everyone was out in the west pasture and Vicky had run into town. He said you answered the call. Even though you were only eleven, you jumped on Dee, galloped out there and drove Shelia back to the main house." Cindi cuddled Peaches against her chest. It was easy to picture this dashing man as the brave, young kid she'd heard all about. "The doctor didn't make it, but at least Lucy's dad had

71

reached the house by the time you returned. If you hadn't met him there, who knows what would have happened."

"Shelia still sends me a Christmas card every year." He sighed and nodded. "I can't believe how big Danny is."

"He's a nice boy. JD let him drive a tractor for the first time last week." She didn't realize she'd rocked the kitten to sleep until Sam's eyes tracked her soft swaying. "He's been talking about applying for his learner's permit as soon as he can next year. You'd have thought it was Christmas around here. Plus he did all the tilling for Jake."

"Holy shit, that makes me feel old." Sam laughed.

The rich baritone caused a flutter in her tummy. "Yeah, right. You're ancient. I mean you must be twenty-four at least."

"Twenty-five." He held up two digits on one hand and all five on the other.

She buried the urge to take his index finger into her mouth. Was she a nympho on top of an exhibitionist? *Jesus.*

"Cindi?"

"Hmm?" She focused her attention on his face once more. Had he gotten even more handsome in the ten seconds that had stretched into an awkward silence? What had he said? Twenty-five. Right. "Old man. You have me by a couple years. I'm twenty-three."

"A babe." A quick wink accompanied his joke. At least she assumed he was joking.

What the hell was she doing standing here flirting with Sam Compton, the last man on earth she should screw around with? "I'd better be heading home."

"Could I ask you something first?" He looked over his shoulder and didn't wait for her to politely decline. "Which stall is Dee in these days?"

"She's next to Couper and Rainey." Cindi crooked her finger as she headed for the prized horses. An easy enough request. She ignored the part of her that had hoped he'd solicit something inappropriate. "Right over here."

Before they'd made it to the gorgeous horse, the mare turned in their direction and scented the air. Cindi often fed her carrots while she took her breaks. Of all the barn residents, she enjoyed Dee the most. JD had encouraged Cindi to take the horse for long rides when the mood struck. Afternoons roaming the ranch never failed to calm her mind.

Dee's nostrils flared and she neighed, rousing the other horses. Cindi crooned to them as Sam jogged the last few steps to his mount.

"Hey, pretty lady." He slid the door open and leaned against the rope stretched across the opening. The horse investigated, huffing as she passed her nose over his face and chest. For an instant, Cindi found herself jealous of the mare.

Sam didn't hesitate to show affection despite his audience of one. He slapped his palm on Dee's shoulder and hugged her neck. He rubbed along the powerful muscles until he could scratch between her ears, then laid a smacking kiss on her nose. "I missed you too."

Cindi's eyes stung at the reunion. "Every couple months an offer comes in on these horses. People telling JD they're too good to waste. Solid figures. I see now why he never considered selling. They're part of your family."

"Yeah." Sam grew quiet. He trailed his fingers around the edge of the star on Dee's nose. "JD's really the glue, isn't he? What's going to happen when he's gone?"

"Your dad's leaving?" Cindi's stomach dropped to the floor.

Sam blinked as if he hadn't heard her.

All thoughts of retreat vanished. Instead she set Peaches on a stack of blankets, then advanced, invading his space. "Is he selling the ranch? Retiring? I never imagined he'd do that. This land is part of him."

"Ah, no." Sam gave Dee one more pat, then stepped into the hallway, snagging Cindi's wrist in the process. Heat infiltrated her suddenly freezing skin. "Fuck. I shouldn't have said anything. Forget I mentioned it, please?"

"As if that's possible." She tried to stifle the panic making her heart beat triple time. "What's happening? Is this why you came home?"

"Sort of." He looked toward the door as if he wished he could make a break for it.

"No, you don't." Cindi gripped his hand. "Sam, you can't leave me hanging."

"It's not my news to share." When his gaze met hers, the misery there knocked the wind from her chest.

Pieces of the puzzle clicked into place. JD's persistent cough. The work he'd done with Colby and even her, transitioning duties he used to own. Silas's rush to dive into the mix even though his injuries should have required another month in bed at least. The arrival of three legends in the span of a single week. Proof stacked too high for her to ignore.

"No." She stumbled backward and would have fallen if Sam hadn't reached out.

"I wasn't thinking." He murmured into her hair as he tucked her close, enfolding her in his arms as though he needed someone to hold on to as badly as she did. "It's still unreal to me. That's not how you should have heard."

"You haven't told me anything." She refused to believe the doomsday scenario screaming in her brain. An odd mix of numbness and violent denial attacked her nervous system. He held her up.

"You know," he groaned.

It couldn't be true.

No. No. No. She shook her head.

"Shit. It's hard to say. Like, if I do, it'll be real." Sam steadied her, himself too, by holding her at arm's length. He spoke soft and clear. "JD has stage three pancreatic cancer. He's d—"

"No!" She fought him then. If he didn't finish uttering that bullshit, maybe it could still be a product of her imagination.

"Shhh." He hugged her to his chest, smothering the flail of her arms. When she couldn't break his hold, she surrendered to the stroking of his fingers through her hair. "So sorry. Shouldn't have done that. Shit. It hurts. I know. Trust me, I know."

Rage alternated with agony and disbelief. She cursed, sobbed and shook her head. Over and over. Not again. She couldn't stand to bury another father. Especially the one who'd loved her most.

Her knees quit supporting her. Peaches scampered from the tumble of their bodies when Sam guided them to the pile of blankets in the corner as though he couldn't manage to stand either.

Cindi didn't give a shit if she'd just met this man. She knew what he was made of, and she needed to borrow some of that strength and integrity. She let him hold her as she cried her heart out on his broad chest. His arms surrounded her. The jerks of his torso echoed hers, and she realized she wasn't the only one breaking down.

Tracing bold swirls across his muscled back helped soothe her pain and the shock of what lie ahead. Every time she thought she might recover enough to untangle herself from his generous embrace, another wave of pain assaulted her.

For JD. For Vicky. For their sons. For herself.

Where would she go from here? What would happen to the ranch? Would JD's sons honor the arrangement she had with their father?

Cindi squirmed from Sam's cradling grasp. She climbed to her feet and dropped her hands to her knees while she caught her breath. A hint of quality cologne flavored each of her pants. She couldn't sort the mixed signals battering her mind.

"I can't believe that just happened." She started to walk away, then turned back as Sam also stood.

He buried his face in the crook of his arm and swiped the moisture from his eyes.

"Did you really say…?"

"Yes." He spun in a flash and kicked a bucket. The metal pail banged as it tumbled down the aisle. "Son of a mother fucking bitch! It's true. JD is dying. *My dad.*"

She couldn't abandon him there, his chest heaving, his cheeks nearly purple and his fists balled at his sides.

This time it was she who offered solace. She approached him with tiny shuffles until they stood toe to toe. He flinched when she settled her fingers over his white knuckles.

Cindi didn't bail. She covered as much of his hands with hers as she could, then massaged the tension from them. "Breathe, Sam. Deep. With me."

The spicy scent of him filled her lungs when she regulated her respiration. After the second inhalation, he began to sync up with her.

"That's right." She sent him a weak, watery smile. "There you go. It's okay to feel however you feel. But fury probably isn't going to help right now. Take another breath. Let it out slow."

He closed his lids as they shared the silence for

another minute or two. When he opened his eyes, they were focused and pure. They complemented his high cheekbones and the golden tones of his skin and hair. "Thanks."

"You're welcome." She stood on her tiptoes for a better view of his face. Their shared grief bonded them together.

His chin dipped as he regarded her more closely.

Cindi yearned to comfort him in the most natural way possible. She licked her lips.

He closed the gap between them.

Her shallow sigh bounced off his lips and buffeted her own face, making her realize exactly how close their mouths had gotten.

She averted her face. "I should go."

He kept possession of her fingers. "Don't."

"Staying isn't wise." *Liar*. Her body ached to linger.

"I know." His dimples deepened. "Do it anyway."

Refusal would have been a knee jerk reaction. Cindi opened her mouth to decline. Instead of a polite rain check, she found herself mumbling her feeble resistance against soft, skilled lips. And by the time she could have separated their mouths and uttered halt, she no longer cared to stop him from transporting her from a nightmare to the fantasy they manufactured together.

She wrapped one leg around his trim hip, assisted by his thick fingers, which supported the crook of her knee. When standing on her tiptoes no longer sufficed, she hopped, trapping him right where she preferred him with her other thigh.

"Mmm." He slid his hands to her ass, cupping her easily in his palms. He guided her, helping her ride his muscled torso as she devoured his exploring tongue. Her back met the worn-smooth wall of the stable when he intensified his barrage of passionate touches.

Friction heated her where his pelvis ground against hers.

Christ, chemistry had never sparked a reaction this strong before. Everywhere she ached, he soothed. Everywhere she burned, he built the flames higher. She touched as much of him as she could reach from the nape of his neck to his impressive shoulders to his back. He leaned into each caress, improving the contact between their bodies.

Some part of her insisted it was wrong to share this level of desperation with a stranger. The pesky voice of reason was drowned out by the storm of their shock and grief as well as the solace they generated in perfect harmony.

Cindi had taken plenty of lovers. A couple of them she'd known no better than Sam. Their reputation had preceded them. She'd trusted Jake to guarantee the men he invited to join in their sessions would respect her. Grounding herself—in this place, in the security of the men who'd adopted her as one of their own—she allowed them to use her as part of their symbiotic exchange. Everyone benefited. For that she owed them more than she could repay.

Still, none had affected her like this. Fun, flirty, dirty—sure.

Imploding in Sam's arms was so much more. So far beyond.

He took what he craved and satisfied her hunger in the same motion.

Cindi snaked her hand between their torsos, relaxing the tension in her legs to allow her room to maneuver. He groaned when she cupped his erection through his jeans.

"Hell yes." His eyes slammed closed for a moment.

She tucked her fingers in his waistband. She

didn't have to reach very far for her prize.

"No underwear? Naughty boy." Cindi giggled when he laughed despite the strain cording his neck and the ghosts haunting his eyes. *More of that. Please.* His contagious mirth buoyed her from the pit of despair threatening to swallow her whole.

"You're the one with your hand in the pants of a guy you barely know."

When she paused, the deficit of sensation seemed to strangle his good humor. "Should I stop?"

He growled and nipped her chin. "You should do what feels right. And, kitten, I have to tell you that feels perfect to me."

"Not too shabby from where I'm hanging either." She hummed as she measured his length with a bold stroke from base to tip. "Very nice."

His grip on her slipped a fraction. She squeaked, then laughed. Relief coated the ulcerous lesions his news had ripped open. What kind of luck did it take to meet the only man who'd ever made her forget all her problems exactly when she needed him most?

How could someone as amazing as Sam be here, with her and available? She shook her head to clear some of the lust so she could form a string of coherent thinking.

"It's okay if this is enough for you." He rubbed his cheek on hers and whispered in her ear, "You're so warm. So different from Belinda. You're bright in my arms. I'm happy to hold you. Kiss you. Like this."

He demonstrated so thoroughly she almost forgot what he'd said. *Belinda.* No matter how she racked her brain, Cindi couldn't recall hearing about someone with the unusual name. If it wasn't a woman from his past… "Slow down a second."

"Too much? Shit, sorry."

She clung when he would have deposited her on

the floor. "No, it's just…"

"Insane?"

"Yeah, that too." She nibbled on him between phrases of her explanation. "I'm wondering if you have a girlfriend—someone you should think about before doing this."

"All I have are a set of bloody claw marks from the beast who stabbed me in the back this morning." He shook his head. "Short answer, no. No one that matters."

"Wow, you really have had a horrible day, haven't you?" She laid her head on his shoulder. "I'm sorry."

He hugged her tight, his arms shaking.

"Nothing you did. In fact, you're proving how little it mattered. Ten minutes or less and I feel closer to you than I did after months of chasing…*her*. I can't even remember her name right now." He drew another sultry kiss from her. "And you? Do I need to be on the lookout for any pissed off cowboys raring to kick my ass? I could use a good fight. Haven't had one in years."

"I'm afraid I'll have to disappoint you." She rubbed the swollen tips of her breasts on his flat chest. Embarrassing or not, she refused to evade the truth. He should make an informed decision. Besides, she didn't care to deal with the ramifications if he found out later. On Compass Ranch, she had no doubt he would hear rumors sooner or later. "I won't lie, Sam. I take lovers. You're not the only one who was with someone earlier today. No one who requires an exclusive claim, though."

Cindi stared into his eyes, daring him to reject her. His rock-solid erection, squeezed gently in her hand, throbbed instead of wilting.

"You had another guy tonight?" His pupils

dilated, and he breathed deep against the curve of her neck. "I think I can smell him."

Them, Sam. Them.

"Does that bother you?" No excuses would pass her lips.

"Fuck, no. I must be more screwed up than I thought. The idea of you with two men... Damn. Is he still around?" The feral glow of his eyes had shivers running up and down her spine. What if Sam had joined their group?

Cindi swallowed three times. Her voice deserted her.

Instead of responding, she shook her head. Negative.

"Too bad."

He must have detected her enormous sigh of relief.

"Don't worry. I'm not looking to tie myself down again. You're safe with me." He grinned. "Unless you believe it's possible to overdose on orgasms?"

"No." She chuckled as she unbuttoned his pants. "Never had that problem before."

"Me either, but we can try our best. In that case..." Sam knelt on the pile of blankets and laid her on her back.

In less than ten seconds he'd stripped himself bare.

Chapter Six

"Holy cow." It didn't make Cindi proud, but she stared. Had she ever seen a man as handsome as Sam Compton outside of the movies? Definitely not.

"Thanks." He beamed as he tugged her blouse over her head and shoved her skirt up around her waist, eying her bare breasts. "I could say the same."

He petted her softly rounded abdomen above the loose cloth. She wished she'd spent as much time as he obviously had at the gym. Not that he seemed to mind. His reverent stroking lulled her.

Without the furnace of his body snugged against her, the night air chilled her skin. Her nipples beaded, firming until they begged to be rubbed. Cindi arched her spine.

"Is this what you would like?" His lips curved against her breast. A teasing kiss landed on the top swell of the left mound.

"Evil." She moved her hand, intending to take care of business herself. The last time she'd come without manual manipulation to supplement her lovers' touches, she'd been sixteen and over the moon for Bobby McAldon, who'd dumped her the day after stealing her virginity. At least he'd taught her a valuable lesson in exchange for a thin sliver of her body.

She'd traded much more for security since then.

"No, wicked would be if I took what you're offering, then abandoned you without returning the favor. I don't plan to disappoint." He slid lower, planting kisses on her hip, then her inner thighs. "Let me make up for…what I did. How you found out."

"It's not your fault." She rubbed the crown of his skull. "The facts aren't any more or less true because you informed me JD is—"

Oh God, could it be true? It hadn't sunk in completely yet.

A fresh sob bubbled from within.

"Shh." He rained sympathy over her in a flurry of licks, kisses and gentle caresses. The more he calmed her, the deeper into their spell he seemed to fall. Knotted muscles in his shoulder melted as he devoted himself to her pleasure.

Cindi closed her eyes and relaxed. Her knees drifted open.

He didn't hesitate to nestle between them. "So pretty."

She zeroed in on the humming vibration that grew stronger with every trip of her pulse. Sam conducted the energy, intensifying it with bold probes of his blunt digits at her entrance. He dipped his head and swiped his tongue through the moisture gathering there.

She yelped when he jerked and cursed.

"Sorry." His groan seemed two octaves deeper. "It caught me off guard, that's all. I can taste the latex on your skin."

"Oh." Her cheeks burned. After several years of unconditional acceptance at Compass Ranch, she worried about perceptions again. Would he think her a slut? How could he not? Would he take her anyway? Hell, maybe it would be easier for him to fuck her if he thought she did this with every man she met. Suddenly, she didn't think she could stand it if he deserted her there, on the soft blanket covering the ground. Naked. Alone. Unfulfilled. She wouldn't hold it against him, though. "I understand if that's...too much."

She lowered her hand and tipped his chin upward. The seal between his mouth and her pussy broke, eliminating the risk of misunderstanding the desire in his stare.

"Are you kidding?" He dropped his forehead on her tummy and breathed deep. "I almost lost it over here. It's hot. Picturing you with another guy. Sexy. I love that you're not closed-minded. Wild as a summer storm. Honest about your needs. It's refreshing."

"Are you sure?"

"Let go of me, and I'll show you." He didn't waste a single heartbeat. The moment her fingers released his face he dove into the saturated folds and worshiped her.

His eager dedication amplified her arousal. When he pressed two fingers inside her and accompanied the slow circular motion he initiated with the swirl of his tongue around her clit, she nearly exploded.

"Not quite yet." He retracted his skilled tongue. "Savor it, Cin. Build it up, then come on my face."

"You'd better stop talking if you mean that." She squirmed, trying to align his mouth where she preferred.

"Then again, if you come quickly I can always take you there again and again." He punctuated each promise with a flick of his tongue in the spot guaranteed to shatter her. Funny how Jake had never noticed. Not that he was a bad partner, not at all, but he didn't seem to have Sam's instinct. No man she'd been with had made love to her like he did.

Raw and earthy with a razor-sharp edge of skill, he startled her with his precision.

Pressure built. The rings of her channel hugged his fingers, which rocked inside her with slow and patient progress. Several minutes of similar treatment spiraled her closer and closer to the pinnacle. She fought tumbling over the edge. Falling from higher up would prolong the ride down.

She could resist the temptation of his lips. But when he walked his free hand up her side, searching for a connection, she cried out. Their fingers entwined.

He squeezed. Tilting his head to the side, he murmured, "Yeah, you're there. Come for me, Cindi. Show me how much you enjoy me lapping at this pretty pussy. Scream so I know how much harder I make you come than the guy you had before."

Dirty talk triggered the initial waves of her climax. The Hoover action of his mouth, accented with the flutter of his tongue on her clit, inspired ordinary release to blossom into something epic. She did more than scream. She broke down and begged.

For more.

For him to stop before she shattered into a million pieces.

She hadn't quite regained use of her limbs when he slithered up her frame. His cock thudded onto her belly and he rocked, gliding it through the wetness he'd inspired. "Please tell me you have another condom somewhere around here."

She couldn't breathe well enough to explain so she flopped her arm toward the mini-purse she'd dropped in the hay nearby.

"Thank God." He dove for the wristlet, then withdrew a foil packet from inside without commenting on the entire strip she had tucked in the zipped pocket.

"Can I?" Cindi loved the endless moment where time suspended and she sheathed a proud man turned beggar, who rushed to bury his length inside her.

"Be my guest." Sam sat on his haunches, allowing her free rein. Effortless. Everything about him amazed her with its natural fit. They complemented each other.

She stroked him several times, pumping up the last bit of stiffness he could muster. Delicious.

"Want to see a trick?" She winked when his jaw fell open.

"Now probably isn't the best time for a magic show unless you want to see my stamina make a great escape." His chest bellowed beneath the force of his pants. Purple and defined, his cock yearned for attention.

"I trust you to keep it together, cowboy."

"I'm glad one of us has faith." A grimace crossed his gorgeous lips. "You're the finest woman I've seen up close and personal. Sweet and filthy. What more could a guy ask for?"

"Most prefer demure and exclusive."

"You haven't lied to me that I know of." He reached out. She evaded his touch. "That's all that matters to me, Cin. Honest passion."

The wry twist of his grin convinced her the woman he'd spoken of earlier had done some serious damage. Maybe Cindi could distract him from the pain for a little while longer.

She popped the condom into her mouth—she always bought the mint variety—then descended toward his stiff cock.

"Oh hell, no."

She glanced up, but he didn't try to stop her.

Instead it was admiration, awe and amusement

she read in his steamy green eyes. Laughing in bed with her partner never failed to turn her on. "You're killing me."

The saying struck a little too close to home. They both froze.

"Shit. Didn't think…"

She tucked the condom against her cheek to reassure him.

"How could you when I'm dazzling you with my sword swallowing?" She wiggled her brows, then enveloped the head of his cock with her mouth, sure to employ every talent she possessed in an attempt to distract him as much as he had her. When he bucked against the tight ring of her lips, snug against his balls, she admitted playtime had to come to a close. Soon. Either that or she'd miss what promised to be the ride of a lifetime.

Her hands choked his shaft while she aligned the rubber with her tongue and proceeded to unfurl the protection, careful to avoid nicking it with her teeth. After his entire length had been coated, she ejected him from her throat and pulled off until he escaped with a pop.

"Brava." The compliment came complete with a standing ovation from his cock.

"My turn." He pounced, driving her to the blankets hard enough to stir up a puff of hay dust. "This one's a disappearing act. Watch my cock vanish inside you."

Cindi laughed and wrapped her hand around his neck.

She tugged him lower so they could kiss while he introduced his body to hers. The simple exchange became anything but when he took the clash of their mouths to the next level. What had he been through that he gobbled her simple display of affection like a starving man? She whispered against his parted lips, "You're full of surprises."

"What's that supposed to mean?" He grew still, peering into her eyes. For a moment, he seemed vulnerable. What kind of scars had his lover left?

"I've studied that picture of you in the grey suit— the Armani—on Vicky's refrigerator. I wondered about all of you. Your brothers, you know. You all seem so different and yet the same. But something about that picture... I don't know. JD even teased me about it a few times." She would have averted her gaze, but he deepened his next kiss.

"Like what you saw?" He licked her bottom lip.

"Hell, yes. Though I never imagined your sense of humor. The light-hearted side of you makes the serious parts even more smoking." She couldn't stop herself. She slid her hands over his ribs, then up his back. "And your passion. Unpretentious pursuit of pleasure. Mmm. A picture might be worth a thousand words, but tonight... This is worth about a million pictures."

"You'd better believe I'm freezing this moment in my memory. A keepsake for when things turn rough." He cradled her shoulders in his hands and pinned her as he flexed his abs and drove his pelvis forward. "I'll remember this."

They both moaned when he sank the barest bit inside her pussy.

"Tell me if I'm hurting you." He rested his forehead on hers, studying her expression for the slightest hint of discomfort. "It's not uncommon for me to have to take things slow."

Cindi breathed through the sting that followed his claiming. He stretched her gently, until his entire length burrowed between her soaked walls. Even then he didn't initiate his strokes. He teased her with innocent kisses over her cheeks and closed eyelids until she couldn't stand it anymore.

"Fuck me, Sam." She arched off the ground, straining to force him to move. "Please."

"Would you mind if I didn't?" The arch of his brows made it seem like he was pleading too.

"Huh?" The weight of him impaling her made her sure she'd misunderstood.

"I'd rather make love to you, Cindi. Play with you." He plumped her breast, drawing circles on his own chest with her nipple. "It's been so long. I forgot what this feels like."

"I'm not sure I've ever known." Ignoring the alarm bells ringing in her mind, she nodded, brushing her lips over his. "I'd like to try it. With you. Tonight."

"I think we already have." His ass lifted as he withdrew a fraction of his length. "A little more. As much as we can stand, okay?"

"Mmm, yes." She crossed her ankles behind his back, limiting his movement. They stayed close, flexing and releasing the pressure on each other. Instead of long, frenzied strokes, they enjoyed the intimacy of full body contact, slow grinds and deep penetration. He held her close, comforting her with the rocking of their bodies.

All the while, he stared into her eyes.

When she hugged him tighter to her chest, he sighed.

"Thank you." He melted over her, conforming to the hills and valleys of her body. "God, I needed this so much. Needed you. Didn't even know it."

She sighed. With him blanketing her, the world couldn't attack her with unfortunate bombshells. She'd had enough of those to last a lifetime.

Compared to the Band-Aid sleeping with Jake and the cowboys applied over her wounds, sharing with

Sam seemed like revolutionary treatment. He prodded something deep within her, bringing it to life, setting her on fire.

Words couldn't do it justice. So instead she used her hands, her lips and the rest of her body to communicate for her. Desperation sped her caresses as they raced toward the inevitable conclusion of their joining. Something so luminous couldn't last forever. It had to burn out in a spectacular display sooner or later.

"Are you close, kitten?" he asked through gritted teeth.

"Right there." She smothered him with shaking arms.

"Me too." He buried his face against her neck and swore.

"Stop fighting it, Sam." If she held him any tighter she might crack his ribs. "I'm with you. You're not alone."

"Neither are you." He tangled his fingers in her hair and kissed the shit out of her.

His hips pumped beneath her heels, and his cock pulsed.

Cindi wished she could feel him shooting his come against the engorged tissue of her pussy. She never allowed herself that luxury. Safety came first, especially when she took multiple partners. *What if...*

Ecstasy rewired her brain. Dreams of one man, this man, infiltrated her wildest fantasies.

Or even better, she imagined him fucking her while the rest of the ranch hands cheered them on.

She screamed.

She quaked.

She lost all sanity and flew into the strongest orgasm of her life.

Through the never-ending spasms, Sam held her. Sheltered her. Lifted her higher.

Colors flared, then dimmed, accompanying the enormous release they shared.

Soothing nonsense filtered through the sated haze in her mind. How long they lay, tangled, she couldn't guess. When the barn came into focus around her once more, he had slipped from her grasp and was disposing of the used condom. Reality smacked her hard.

Did she regret what they'd done? No. How could she?

But would it make things more difficult in the coming months? Exponentially.

She scrounged around for her clothes, keeping her gaze averted from his sculpted body so she wouldn't be tempted for a rematch. The silk of her blouse had barely settled onto her shoulders when he approached, fully clothed.

"Stay with me tonight." It wasn't a question.

"Here? In the barn? And tell the guys what when I'm wearing the same clothes tomorrow?" They would notice since they'd peeled them from her earlier. She couldn't help the widening of her eyes. What had she done?

The ramifications were potentially endless. Jake flashed into her mind. He already harbored some serious bitterness toward Sam. That much had been clear this afternoon. If he found out, if it seemed like anything more than a physical outlet, it wouldn't end well.

"Come to the main house." He played with her fingers as though he couldn't stand to let her go. Somehow the gesture struck her as sweet instead of needy. At least he hadn't tucked himself in his pants and run off. He acted as if their sharing meant something more than a casual roll in the hay. Whether she admitted it—to him, herself or the universe—it'd been bigger than that to her too.

"And what do you think Vicky and JD will have to say about that? Maybe I could sneak out the window like a naughty teenager at the crack of dawn?" She blew a derisive laugh through her delightfully swollen lips. "No, thank you."

"Cindi—"

"I can't." She tried again to free her hand and failed. "And neither can you, Sam. Your family needs you. Distractions or some kind of crazy drama would be unfair to pile on top. There's enough of that going around with Silas and the girl, Jody, that Seth told me a little about. We have to be responsible. Do the right thing. For everyone. I won't jeopardize my position here. Not for anything. Or anyone."

"Smarter than me." He shook his head despite his frown. Then he stroked the pad of his thumb across her knuckles. "I didn't see any extra cars in the yard. Do you need a ride?"

"I'll walk." One of her hands broke loose. Regret swamped her, keeping her from tugging too hard on the other.

"To where?" His eyebrows rose. "It's after midnight for Christ's sake. And it's miles to the main road."

"I live here." It stung a little that he didn't know that.

"In the barn?" The green of his eyes was even nicer when Sam opened them wide.

"No." She couldn't stop the laugh that burst from her chest. "You must really be tired. I stay in your great aunt Meade's cottage."

"I thought that old thing would have fallen down by now."

"Probably would have if we hadn't restored it." Cindi adjusted the angle of her hand as they stood shoulder to shoulder. She edged toward the moonlight streaming through the open barn door. Their fingers wove together, unwilling to sever their connection so soon.

It felt too nice to shake loose before she had to.

"Still, that's at least a half-mile over the ridge." He frowned. "You're not hiking out there alone, upset, sleepy. No way."

"Who do you think you are to make decisions for me?" She glared up at him. "You don't even know me. Just because we—"

"It wouldn't matter who you were. It's not safe."

How could she argue with his chivalrous tendencies? Futile effort if he was anything like JD.

"Look, I understand if you don't want to be alone with a stranger... I mean, me, out there." He drew her closer to his side, intentionally or not. "I'll call Colby. How's that?"

Reality was, she could hardly consider him a new acquaintance after the life-altering moment they'd shared. Sometimes tragedy formed an instant bond that transcended individuals and called on their basic humanity. Like the night she'd watched footage of the tsunami destroy entire villages in Japan on the black and white TV on the counter inside Compton Pass's only twenty-four hour gas station. Her late-night ice cream melted—utterly forgotten—in her hands. She hadn't known the woman in the blue sweater behind her, but that hadn't stopped them from hugging as the buildings collapsed and families washed away.

JD had been her personal foundation. He'd helped her find her place in life. To share the pain of losing him with his son... Well, she could only hope she'd helped the suave businessman as much as he'd comforted her.

"Don't wake the foreman." She shook her head. "Silas won't rest without him home after the fiasco the other night. He needs his sleep to heal. Especially considering...everything else."

"Then you're stuck with me." Sam had inherited his father's headstrong nature.

"Fine. But you can't come inside." A little of the quality had rubbed off on her in the past two years.

"Deal. I'll escort you as far as the top of the hill. Okay?"

She nodded.

They strolled beneath the stars in silence, though he held her hand the entire journey. Suddenly she wished she lived a million miles away. The cricket song, the breeze in the long grass and the hint of water bouncing through the creek on the way to the pond all lulled her with nocturnal tranquility.

How could nature not mourn as she did?

The night should smell foul—like rotten carcasses—instead of fresh, perfumed with grass and asters.

With every step, Sam relaxed beside her. His thumb brushed over her knuckles when he helped her hop the tree that had fallen during the last summer storm. She hadn't bothered to mention it to JD or Colby since they'd both been so busy lately.

When the slate roof of her home popped into view, she paused.

Sam turned toward her and dusted a tendril of hair from her cheek.

Cindi couldn't say if she was upset or glad when he didn't try to take it beyond that.

"Go ahead," he whispered. "I'll wait here until you're inside."

"Sam, I—" There were so many things she would have liked to say. She opted for simplicity. "Thank you, and I'm sorry."

He nodded. "It was nice to meet you, Cindi

Middleton."

"Same goes. I only wish the circumstances had been better."

"Me too." He tipped his jaw toward the cottage. "Sweet dreams. Call the house if you need anything. I'll be there."

"You can feel free to do the same." She blushed. "You know, if you need to talk."

He impressed her when he resisted instinctive denial. "I may just do that."

"Anytime. Sam."

"Yeah?" He perked up, but didn't crowd her personal space.

"When we see each other tomorrow." She swallowed hard. It would be nearly impossible. She'd do it if she had to. "Let's pretend this never happened."

"Why make things awkward, right?"

"Exactly." A weak smile covered her disappointment.

"I appreciate that, Cin." He nodded. "My focus has to be on JD."

"Mine too. And the future."

"Understandable. Goodnight."

"'Night, Sam." They stood there, staring at each other for a few more seconds. His glittering eyes dazzled her, but still… "Could you let go of my hand now?"

"Sure. Yeah. That would probably help." He lifted her knuckles to his lips and laid a gentle kiss on the inside of her wrist before unknitting their fingers.

If she didn't act fast, she'd succumb to the offer in his eyes. They would drift down onto the long, soft grass, and she would convert a difficult situation into a damn near impossible one.

Too risky.

Cindi picked a route she had memorized across

the meadow with more concentration than the trek required. She prided herself on not glancing backward until she'd fit her key in the lock on the back door. Thank God she hadn't given in to temptation before then or she might have dashed up the hill and tackled the figure silhouetted on the horizon.

She could have used him to sear away the darkness in her heart, which was so much blacker than the gorgeous midnight they'd shared.

Chapter Seven

Sam toyed with the stem of his wineglass at dinner the next night. He glanced around the table, comparing the bottles of beer in front of Colby and Seth, Vicky's wine cooler, the tumbler of whiskey his father nursed and the tall glass of iced tea beside Silas's plate. Lucy sipped vitamin-enriched water in some pink, faux-fruit flavor. What had seemed like insurmountable differences when he was younger felt like welcome diversity after his return home.

They had all the important things in common, starting with their unconditional support of each other. He would bet that if Cindi had accepted JD's invitation to dinner, she'd have been a pinot noir drinker like him. Or maybe she would have joined him in a flute of Cristal. Not that he cared one way or the other.

He shook his head to clear his thoughts of the woman he'd shared comfort-slash-rebound sex with during their one night stand and focused on the important things in his life. The enduring things.

Members of his family ringed the table with conversation and laughter. Content to absorb their positive energy, Sam half-listened. JD discussed a problem they were having—something to do with one of the ranch hands and suspected petty theft—with Silas and Colby. Vicky and Lucy laughed about local gossip regarding the preacher's wife and one of the less devout members of the congregation. Seth hopped from one conversation to the other, interjecting wise-ass remarks.

They were finishing up their meal when the doorbell rang.

"Damn. Who visits at suppertime?" JD grumbled, rising slowly.

Not to mention anyone they knew wouldn't bother with the chime. Hell, Sam hadn't remembered they *had* a doorbell. The Compton household was more of a knock-and-enter operation. Sometimes more of an enter-and-holler-hello facility to be honest.

"I'll get it," he offered. JD waved his hand so Sam plopped into his seat again. Last thing he wanted was to baby his dad.

"Naw. I'm the closest." JD disappeared into the hallway. Conversation resumed. Silas and Colby filled Seth and Sam in on some of the more recent improvements that had been made to the ranch. It would take a while to ramp up his understanding of how things worked these days.

It wasn't long before JD reappeared. "Uh, Seth. Maybe you should come out here, son."

Sam whipped his stare to his brother. Thank God it was Seth on the receiving end of that bewildered glance from their father and not Sam. Usually unflappable, JD started to say something more, then choked on his comment.

Sam couldn't recall ever having seen him at a loss before.

"Oookay." Seth drew out his assent as he rose slowly.

Sam joined the rest of the family, trailing Seth as

he ambled toward the front foyer as though stalking through a haunted house where ghosts or zombies might tear him limb from limb at any moment.

Sam could say they had his back. The truth of the matter was they were nosy.

Seth stopped short. The rest of the family jammed up. Vicky bumped into JD. Sam was knocked into his mom when Colby and Lucy bounced into him and Silas avoided the mess as he hobbled along in the rear.

"Who is *she*?" Lucy gasped as she strained to see around the three men in front of her. Si whispered in the background, filling his lovers in.

Sam had no question. The sassy woman sporting an antique lace wedding dress was none other than Jody Kirkland. Even with her clothes on, he couldn't mistake the fire in her eyes. Forget a bee in her bonnet, the girl had a whole wasp's nest under that skirt.

Poor Seth.

His brother didn't make things any better for himself when he quipped, "Nice dress."

Careful, bro. Sam wanted to shout out a warning.

The family listened as Jody and Seth weaved through a series of misunderstandings and wounded pride that put "Who's on First" to shame.

Sam sucked in a pained breath when Seth dropped to one knee and proposed. He remembered his intentions to make that same gesture for Belinda. Watching the couple before him now, he realized he'd never had that unconditional love. Not for or from any woman.

Cindi's face flashed through his memory. Until he remembered how quick she'd been to dismiss what they'd shared. When JD had introduced them earlier, she'd smiled politely and shook his hand as though they hadn't damn near burned the barn down last night.

At least his brothers had brighter futures.

Jody accepted Seth's proposal. The tired, drawn expression Seth had worn since Sam landed in Wyoming disappeared, replaced by sheer, unadulterated happiness. Sam couldn't help but be swept away by their bliss. He whistled and clapped. His brothers were the luckiest bastards on the face of the earth. After missing his shot, or two, he couldn't be happier for them.

"Well, hot damn." JD whooped. "Looks like we got a wedding to look forward to."

Sam figured Seth had the same thought he did when his brother ended his lip lock prematurely. Jody blinked in surprise at his quick retreat.

"I wanna get married right away." Time wasn't on JD's side. If it were Sam, he'd do anything necessary to ensure their father was present on the big day. "No long engagement."

Jody laughed and pointed to her dress. "Sweetheart, if there was a minister here, I'd marry you tonight."

"Oh no," Vicky cried out, rushing over to where Seth and Jody stood. "I want a proper wedding. We can hold it right here at the ranch. Lots of flowers and friends and a big-ass party afterward."

Jody turned to Vicky, grinning. "That sounds terrific."

Seth introduced them all to his new fiancée. By the time she'd made the rounds, Sam felt sure their family had grown in the matter of an evening. Jody talked shop with JD, shared the grief she'd endured as a woman on a male-dominated ranch with Lucy and Vicky and gave as good as she got from Sam and Silas over the whole webcam incident. She fit seamlessly with the group, something Belinda never would have been able to accomplish.

When Seth and Jody headed upstairs to

reconnect, Sam ducked outside.

He hated the jealousy he couldn't ignore as it clawed at his guts. How could he ever find someone who fulfilled both sides of his nature—sophisticated yet down to earth? No fancy woman would settle for this life, would she?

Maybe he had his priorities completely fucked up. A steady woman like Lucy or Jody would be a blessing. Sweet, funny and caring, they'd satisfy him most of the time.

No relationship could be perfect, right?

He flopped into the porch swing and planted his boot on the rail, rocking a bit faster than was probably recommended. After stewing a good, long while, the chill of the evening began to register. He chafed his arms, then prepared to head inside.

A sliver of light grew across the yard, drawing his attention before it flicked into darkness when someone shut off the barn lamps, then closed the big sliding door. A figure, too petite for any of the ranchers, blended with the shadows. He didn't think Cindi had spotted him until she lifted one hand in a meager wave.

He mimicked her greeting.

For a single moment he debated trotting after her like a lost puppy. He stood. From this distance he couldn't be sure, but he thought she might have smiled. Then he remembered how oblivious she'd seemed to the current racing up his arm when their palms had met in that disgustingly courteous shake earlier in the day.

Enough chasing his tail already.

Enough being led by his cock.

Enough caring for women who didn't have more in mind than a world-class fuck or to fuck him over, however that went.

Sam planted his feet and crossed his arms over his chest.

The posture didn't prevent his sigh when she walked away. Nor did it stop the breath that stuck beneath his ribs when she did a one-eighty.

Cindi faced him and stared for a solid ten seconds before marching up to the porch.

Unwilling to give her leverage, Sam sank onto the swing again, settling his old hat over the instant hard-on testing the strength of his jeans.

"Hi." She paused at the top of the stairs.

"Howdy."

"Mind if I join you?" It was more than a polite inquiry. She'd vanish if he asked her to. Tempted, he couldn't take the easy path when she worried her plump bottom lip.

"Of course not." The truth overrode his need to save face. "Have a seat."

Sam slid to one side, but the swing dictated their coziness. His nostrils flared when their thighs pressed together.

They rocked in silence, staring out at the ranch for a bit.

"JD came to talk to me today." She monitored the never-ending effort of a moth, which flew repeatedly into the bulb illuminating the stairs.

Buzz. Crash. Buzz. Crash. Buzz.

Sam couldn't help himself either. He laid his hand on top of Cindi's trembling fingers.

"Thanks." She swallowed hard. "I'm so glad you gave me a heads-up. I mean, I didn't tell him you did. But I had a chance to organize my thoughts beforehand. I think I muddled through okay. I focused on him instead of…"

"Your broken heart." Ah, fuck it. Sam released the tension in his neck, allowing his face to angle toward the gravitational force of her sweetness laced with suffering.

"Yeah." She sniffled, though the sobs of the night before didn't resurface. Thank God. His chest still ached from the force of her misery. And his own. "I owe you. For letting me be supportive instead of selfish. The shock… If I hadn't had a chance to process the news, it would have gone differently. I was proud of how I held it together. Above all, I couldn't stand myself if I added to his pain."

"I'm glad to be of service." He stared into her wide eyes, then laughed. "And that sounded totally sketchy. Didn't mean it like—"

"Like you'd be willing to throw me a bone every time I'm having a bad day?"

They both cracked up then. Damn, she was easy to hang around. Nothing like the snippy indignation Belinda had shot at him every time he opened his mouth.

Her smile tempted him to taste it. Somehow he resisted. Something more attractive than the potent sexual connection they shared inspired him to abstain. "Look, Cindi—"

"You don't owe me any explanations." She covered his mouth with two fingers.

"Maybe not, but I'd like to give you one anyway. If you don't mind listening."

"I, uh, realize we sort of just met. Still, I hope you believe I'm here for you like you were for me. Whenever you need someone, Sam." She squeezed his knee. "I'm a pretty decent friend."

He stifled a groan both at her touch and the infamous platonic reference every man loathed. Except that's what he hoped for in this case. Wasn't it?

"I appreciate that." He nodded. "Things don't have to be awkward between us. We're both adults. Last night was great. Exactly what I—no, *we*—needed. I just thought you should know I'm not looking for anything…more."

"Same here." A frown chased relief from her face. "The woman you mentioned yesterday. Belinda. She betrayed you. JD isn't the only reason you came home, true?"

Women's intuition never ceased to amaze him. "Yeah."

"Well, I'm nothing like that bitch. You can be sure of that."

"Believe me, I know." Sam chuckled. Belinda would never have gone wild in the dusty barn. Hell, she probably wouldn't have set a single Prada-clad foot in the place. No need to rub Cindi's face in the discrepancy. High-priced and high-class swapped places in his estimation.

She tilted her head but didn't ask him to explain.

Somehow, her hands-off approach made him spill his guts.

By the time he'd recounted the gory details, Cindi's cheeks had gone purple. "And you're not going to fight?"

"For what?" He scratched his chin. "My job? Hell, no. They don't deserve me. My pride? No point. She fooled me with her act. I had it coming."

"I wouldn't say that. How about your reputation?" She stroked her thumb over the back of his hand.

"The people who count would never have believed her lies." Sam stared into her eyes, hoping he could include her in that category.

"After a single day I couldn't have taken her seriously." Cindi laid her head on his shoulder. "I'm sorry your bosses let you down. They were too chickenshit to see beyond her petty games. In those circles, scandal rules. Even the threat of one can be deadly. Rumors cause as much damage as fact. If they had merited your loyalty, none of that would have mattered, though. They would have stuck by you and damn the consequences."

Sam wondered how she knew. "Thanks."

"I guess there's only one thing for you to do." She patted his thigh.

"What's that?" He raised his eyebrows.

"Kick their asses. Rake in the cash they could have made with you by their sides." Her devious laugh had his cock throbbing. "Hit them where it hurts. Right in their big fat wallets."

He hadn't expected her to understand. "I made my first buy this afternoon."

"Atta boy." She lifted her head and wiggled her brows at him. "Maybe you should give me some stock tips. I'd be glad to help. In the name of our new friendship of course."

"Mighty generous, Cin." He laughed. Too bad the commodities he'd picked up had such an enormous cost per share. Otherwise, he might have taken her up on the offer. No need to rub her face in the high stakes he'd operated with in his old world.

"I do what I can."

They stared into each other's eyes.

What she'd done—for him, to him, with him—last night tempted him to fish for a repeat performance. Except ruining their budding friendship wasn't something he was willing to risk. Not even for phenomenal sex.

Sam stood abruptly and she followed suit.

"I guess I'd better go." She nodded toward a beat-up Ford in the drive. "Brought my truck tonight."

"Drive safe." What were the odds the thing wouldn't start and he could usher her through the Indian paintbrush and bluebells again? Probably too much to ask of the universe.

"Will do. Goodnight, Sam." She rose onto her tiptoes. Soft lips seared his skin though she only pecked his stubbly cheek.

"Goodnight." He stood on the porch until the rattle of her better-days ride faded into the night. Then he pivoted on his boot heels and hustled inside before the loneliness smothering him convinced him to do something stupid.

Something like chasing her down, then scooping her onto Dee's back and racing them out to one of the many secluded spots on the ranch for a night of getting to know each other better, whether that meant by talking or by touching. Only a fool would ask for that kind of punishment so soon after taking a beating.

Silas and Seth had known who their forever partners were from the time they were teenagers.

He wished he could say the same.

Then again, maybe there was no such thing for him. Screwing around with the wrong women meant damning himself to frustration and regret, time after time.

Better to sleep alone.

The kitchen door banged behind him, punctuating his retreat.

"Sam!" Vicky hollered from her room on the first floor.

"Sorry, Ma." He didn't dare go upstairs. Falling into his bed, which shared a wall with Seth's, would only doom him to eavesdropping on his brother's happily ever after in progress. Instead, he snagged his laptop off a coffee table in the living room and headed for the back porch.

Maybe he'd tinker with his portfolio and see what kind of damage he could do from across the country. No reason why he couldn't implement some of his stolen strategies to pass the time. Making money always took his mind off the things he might be missing out on, at least temporarily.

Seven weeks and five days until Sawyer hit dry land and he had someone to commiserate with. It would take a hell of a lot of profit to last that long.

Chapter Eight

One week later

Sam had avoided the barn for a week, ever since his first night home. But if he stared at the Dow's neon green ticker blipping across his damn computer screen a minute longer he'd go nuts. He'd already mastered three point shots on the Nerf basketball net taped to the back of the porch door and built a paperclip statue worthy of the MOMA.

The promise of a few hours roaming the ranch on horseback called to him. After all, he had some time to kill. Opening a new fund and putting his research into play had seemed like a worthy challenge. Except it'd gone remarkably well. So well, he didn't have a hell of a lot to do as he let the research he'd slaved over for months pay off.

Without the bullshit of corporate existence, like producing standardized reporting half the recipients didn't bother to open or devoting an entire day to a presentation partners would flip through in fifteen minutes, while wishing they were anywhere else, he was suddenly far more agile in his trades and better off when it came to work-life balance.

The availability at decent prices of the stock he had planned to recommend also surprised him. Had Belinda not yet traded for Smith, Winfield and Gandle? What were they waiting for?

While he speculated, he'd rearranged the entire porch, reconfiguring it into a pleasant office filled with plants, sunlight and memories of the nights he'd camped out on the floor with his brothers. Swapping his impersonal glass and chrome space for the dinged up old couch would do. This morning JD had stopped by to check out his handiwork and mentioned an unused desk in the back of the barn. Sam figured he might as well lug it up to the main house and add it to his space before the novelty of lounging on the sagging cushions mutated into a sore back.

At least those were all the reasons he justified his visit to the barn. Problem was, he'd searched every place he could think of, including the loft where he'd lost his virginity to Brandi Morrone, and had no luck locating the furniture.

He knew exactly who to ask about the desk since he'd bet it used to be hers before JD upgraded her workstation. Pretending he didn't ache to visit with the cute bookkeeper would be ridiculous in any case. He wondered how she was coping. Vicky wouldn't approve of his manners in not checking up on her, would she?

Quick in, quick out. A little chatting never hurt anybody.

As long as he stuck to common courtesy and ignored the fantasies he'd spent the last several afternoons dreaming up, things would work out. It wasn't as if Cindi would consent to him ravishing her during the middle of the day while she had a job to do. Hell, she'd barely acknowledged the connection they'd forged in the seductive twilight they'd shared his first night home when she'd joined them for dinner periodically.

So why had it felt like they'd done a hell of a lot more than console each other or walk hand in hand?

He took a deep breath and swung into her territory.

Cindi sat behind her desk, contorting her face in an expression similar to the one Sam had made as a kid when Sawyer would take his crassness to new levels and fart in their old bunk beds. Somehow he doubted that was the problem here. "Something wrong?"

"Oh!" She jumped, then shook her head. "Damn Googleheimer's."

"Excuse me?" He squinted, as though the clarity could help him understand her better.

"You know…when you open a browser and forget what you planned to look up on the Internet." She smiled.

"Ahh, of course. Happens all the time." He chuckled, then leaned his upper thigh against her desk until he could sneak a glimpse at her screen. "What I do to combat Googleheimer's is rewind my brain."

"It's not exactly a DVR up here." She tapped her temple with one perfectly manicured fingernail. How did she manage that while working in a barn?

"What were you thinking about before you opened the window?"

"I can't remember." She bit her lip. "Shit."

"Okay, plan B." He grinned. "Think of something entirely different. The original thought might spontaneously return to your mind."

"What the—" She started when he dusted her hair back from her temple and nuzzled her neck. He had to help her out, didn't he?

His brain screamed red alert. What happened to gossiping and not touching? Since it was for her own good, he figured he'd write himself a free pass. He breathed deep against her skin.

"God damn you smell even better up close," he whispered in her ear. "Are you wearing *L'Heure Bleue*?"

She faced him so fast he didn't have time to retreat. Their lips nearly brushed when she squeaked, "You know Guerlain? Impressive."

"Not bad for a backward cowboy, huh?"

"Sorry, that came out wrong." She laid a hand on his forearm, infusing more heat into his skin than the subtle contact should have generated. "It's more like most guys don't notice at all."

Sam found that hard to believe.

"I bought a bottle for my ex." *Belinda the Big Apple Bitch.* He stood and ran his hand through his hair, trying not to scowl at the reminder.

"She must have appreciated such a generous gift."

"Hardly." He couldn't keep the bitterness from his laugh. "She hated it. Too *bourgeois* for her."

"Damn." Cindi shook her head. "I'd hate to see her shopping bills."

"No kidding." He didn't mention how Belinda had flown to Paris on chartered jets and hired world-renowned designers for her one-of-a-kind power suits. Mostly on other guys' dimes. No reason to rub Cindi's face in a lifestyle she couldn't possibly hope to have. Still, why shouldn't she benefit from Sam's poor taste in women? God only knew, on her salary, quality perfume had to be a luxury. "The crew in New York is packing up my apartment this weekend. You're welcome to have the bottle when the rest of my stuff arrives."

"Thanks but—"

"I insist." He waved off her objections. Yes, it

was an expensive gift from a near stranger. Too damn bad. For once, he wanted to do something for a woman who'd be grateful for the effort and extravagance of his pampering. "Not like I plan to wear it. It suits you. Very lovely."

She seemed like she might keep arguing.

So he told the truth. "It's either that, or I throw it in the trash. I don't care for any souvenirs. You know what I mean?"

"I do. Thank you, Sam." Why would that, of all things, cause her to blush?

"You're welcome." He leaned closer, maybe for another whiff of the potent blend of Cindi and violets or maybe for something a tad more dangerous.

"Oh my God!" She clapped her hands and bounced. Her breasts distracted him from the elusive something in her gaze that had him thinking bullshit he'd be better off ignoring. Before he could take evasive maneuvers, she threw her arms around his waist and hugged. "You're a genius. I was about to look up a reasonable source for pickup-bed water caddies. Colby wants every truck equipped since the incident."

"What happened?" Sam hated being so out of the loop.

"Jake gave his canteen to one of the new hands who didn't pack enough. He got dehydrated and ended up in the hospital overnight. The fool worked until he dropped. Scared the shit out of Colby and the rest of the guys. They thought he'd had a heart attack. It's a long ride back from the west pasture." Her eyes darkened a shade or two.

Could there be something between her and the cowboy who'd worked Compass Ranch nearly as long as Sam had been alive. Could he be the guy she'd entertained last week? Jake had to be at least ten, maybe fifteen, years older than her. Not that Sam gave a shit.

"I think I'm going to talk to him about limiting JD's time out there too. What if…"

Sam wished he could plug his ears and yell *la la la* like he had when he was a kid and Silas tried to convince him there was no Santa. He didn't realize he'd crossed the space until Cindi's gentle call registered on his mind.

"Sam."

"Yeah." He paused with one foot over the threshold.

"When you're ready and you'd like to talk about it. Well… I'm a good listener." The pity in her gaze turned his stomach. "My door is always open."

"I'm fine. Besides, you don't actually have a door." He waved at the clear air between her office and the main section of the barn.

"Okay." She held her hands up, palm out. "Thanks again. You know, for helping me remember."

"Googleheimer's. Right."

"Hey, did you come in here for something?" Her brows drew together.

He could admit to himself he'd already gotten what he'd really sought. A chance to see her again, smell her again and almost taste her again. Damn it.

"Ah, yeah." He wondered for a moment if there were an analog version of Googleheimer's. He had to scroll back and dig up the shoddy excuse JD had given him to seek out the office manager. "A desk. JD said there's one out here somewhere I can take up to the house."

"Oh." Her lower lip plumped out in a sexy pout.

Could she have hoped for something different?

"Let me show you." She rounded her station and slipped past him. He didn't move out of her trajectory fast enough, and she brushed every inch of his front.

They both drew a huge breath.

Her flirty sundress floated around her as she spun and nearly ran toward the attached shed around the rear of the space. Funny, Sam had specifically asked if that's where it was. JD had assured him it wasn't. Maybe his dad was starting to forget things. Somehow Sam doubted it.

The rancher could be devious when it suited him.

"It's right there." She pointed to the back corner. "Do you want some help digging it out?"

Sam raked his gaze from her elegant up-do to the cream silk ruffles floating around her on the breeze. "Thanks, but not from you. Wouldn't want to muss you up."

"I'm not the kind of woman who minds getting dirty every now and then."

Holy Christ. Could she have meant that like it sounded?

The blush creeping up her chest and neck said no.

Too damn bad.

"No worries. I've got this." He didn't face her again—afraid she'd spot the raging hard-on in his jeans.

It wasn't until later, when he wrestled the solid oak desk off the back of one of the ranch's pickups and up the stairs to the main house, that he wondered where the hell Cindi had come from. Certainly not Compton Pass. He would have remembered someone like her.

Silas hobbled onto the porch with a frosty beer in one hand and his crutch in the other. When Sam set the desk on the porch with a serious grunt, his brother tossed him the bottle.

"None for you?"

"Nah. My drinking days are done." His brother lowered himself to a wicker chair.

"What're you doing back?" Usually the guys stayed out until dinnertime. "Everything all right?"

"Suppose so." Silas grimaced. "My fucking thigh was aching like a bitch. I was slowing them down. Colby noticed and shipped me out. I think I'm more of a distraction anyway. Uh, JD came home with me. He's taking a nap."

"Whoa." Sam hopped up onto the desk, his thighs spread as he chugged half the beer before dangling the brown bottle between his knees.

"I know." Si stared off into the distance. "There's got to be a first time for everything I suppose."

The condensation-coated label resisted Sam's trimmed nails as he picked at the corners. "It freaks me out. Part of me knows it's true, but he's here every day, walking, talking, being a pain in the ass as usual. I can't imagine it's going to happen so soon. That he'll be gone. I honest to God can't picture it. Like when someone tells you how big the universe is and you know it's ginormous. But when you translate the distance from a theoretical model to contemplating the real thing… It just doesn't compute."

"Look, I'm no genius. I never did great in school like you. There was plenty of shit that made no sense to me. I think I get what you're saying, though." His brother sighed. "And I'm okay with not imagining it before I have to if you don't mind. Unless you need to…talk…or something."

Sam laughed. "Don't worry, I won't torture you like that, bro. I'll find someone else if I need to unload. Maybe Lucy or Colby wouldn't mind listening."

"Sorry. I would try for you." Si scrubbed his face. "But they're way better at it than me. Some people have that warm, fuzzy thing going for them, you know? I ain't one of them."

"Being a man of action is valuable too."

"Fat lot of good it does when you're sidelined." A low growl came from his brother's chest. "When they

115

need me most, I'm stuck here like their fucking housewife. Except I can't cook worth a damn."

"Yeah, please leave that to Vicky." Sam frowned. "I never even offered to head out there. Think I should?"

"Uh, no offense." His brother shook his head. "You'd be in the way. Besides, why do something your heart's not in? Isn't that sort of the point of coming back to Compton Pass? You're lending your own kind of support to the family."

They both stared at the desk he sat on.

"JD has good insurance. He's packed away tons. Still, he and Colby have been making a bunch of improvements around here. Investing for the future." Si shrugged. "I'll leave it to you to figure out the cash flow and all that stuff. It might not hurt if you reviewed the books. Help us understand our resources and our limitations. Plus, you could spend some time with sexy Ms. Cindi."

"What do you know about her?" Sam leaned back onto one palm, trying to act casual.

"Son of a bitch. Score another point for Lu." His brother shifted, searching for a comfortable position. "She called it by the second day you were home. Said Cindi's been asking about you too."

"Really?" If submitting to some teasing would distract Si for a few minutes, Sam would take one for the team. It wasn't like he *really* wanted to know more about her.

"Yep. Lucy told her a bunch of stories that made you look cooler than you really are, don't worry." Silas grinned.

"Nice. I'll have to thank her later."

"So…Cindi. Lucy and Colby gave me the run down. You're lucky they're not playing matchmaker yet. Seemed to think you two would hit it off. She's been here a little over two years. Never leaves Compton Pass. Is great at her job. Has been organizing the financials over time. Works hard." Silas cocked his head. "Some rumors that she plays hard too."

"What's that supposed to mean?" Sam couldn't stop replaying the instant she'd told him she didn't mind getting dirty. He figured that revelation was going to keep him occupied in the shower later.

"JD told me she likes to frolic with the cowboys." Silas shrugged. "Still find it hard to believe she has a nasty bone in her body. She's always so perfect looking. Real classy. But it was part of the whole don't-judge-a-book-by-its-cover speech."

The window on the side of the porch creaked as it lifted up.

Shit, JD.

"Should I have added on the keep-private-discussions-to-yourself speech, son?" Their dad busted them big time.

"You always did have a knack for sensing when we were up to no good." Silas grinned.

"'Cause I know what I would have been doing if I were in your shoes." Their dad chuckled. The sound morphed into the hacking cough Sam had come to dread. Except this time it kept worsening until JD had trouble catching his breath.

Sam rushed inside, snagging some water from the refrigerator when soft curses dotted the wheezes floating from the direction of his parents' bedroom.

He hustled down the hall, ignoring the dirt he tracked from his boots. He'd clean it up before Vicky noticed.

"Here, drink this." He handed the bottle to his dad.

The other man's hands seemed too weak to twist the top off. He fumbled twice before Sam sank to the mattress and did it for him. With one arm wrapped around his father's back, he helped JD sit up far enough to take a couple sips.

The fit faded away. After JD breathed easier, Sam laid his father against the pillows, propping him half-sitting against the headboard.

"Be careful." The warning hissed between puffs of breath.

"Did I hurt you?" Sam couldn't imagine damaging the man who could kick anyone's ass with both hands tied behind his back.

"Not me." JD's fingers latched onto Sam's knee, gouging a little. "Careful with little Cin."

"What?" He sputtered. "I haven't... I'm not planning on..."

His dad sighed. "Listen good. I'm not telling you not to follow your heart. Just don't spook her, you hear me?"

"There's nothing in my damn heart." Sam scowled. "I hardly know her."

"I do. I know you both. Enough to tell you I'd be disappointed if you let whatever the hell went wrong in New York make you stupid now, when it counts." JD motioned for another gulp of the water. A trickle of the cool liquid ran down his chin.

Sam mopped it up with the corner of the sheet.

"It's important." JD battled his drooping lids. "She belongs here. Compass Ranch is her home. You can't take that from her. You can't chase her away. Either because you rush her or because you ignore what could be. It would devastate her to lose her family."

"What about her *real* one?" Sam couldn't deny the urge to learn more. "Where are they?"

"Gone. Never were there for her really." JD looked like he would have spit on the ground if they'd had this discussion outside. "They owed her better. Has it now. I'm asking you to look after her. Protect her. Don't let her disappear in the shuffle after I'm gone."

The strength in his dad's grip surprised him when he squeezed Sam's wrist.

"Swear it to me, Sam."

Their stares met and stuck.

"I promise, JD. I'll make sure she's okay."

"Thank you." He finally relaxed, his eyes drifting shut. "Mind closing the shade? I think I'll take that nap after all."

"Sure, Pa."

Chapter Nine

Two weeks after coming to Compass Ranch

Afternoon bitch sessions became one of the highlights of Sam's days. He looked forward to hanging out with Silas and JD, who'd adopted a half-day schedule as their standard. Any other assortment of visitors from town joined in to toss back a few cold beers while spending time with the head of Compass Ranch.

Sam had even managed to convert the old-timers to his favorite microbrew. This casual small-town social phenomenon was something he'd lost entirely in the bustle of his previous world where the most interaction he'd had with his neighbors included a smile in the hallway or weather chat during the elevator ride to the lobby. Reclaiming the tradition felt right. Another step in merging the two halves of his identity.

Today it seemed like he and Silas were the only takers. Too bad Seth and Colby could never join in. Maybe he'd start up a late-night edition of their group when the dust settled a bit. Then all they would need was Sawyer, sitting shoulder to shoulder with them on the porch stairs as he recounted his latest conquests.

"You gonna cave and reach out to him?" Silas nudged Sam's knee and gestured toward his Smartphone.

"Honestly." Sam prepared to dash for the safety of the yard. "I already did. A few times."

"And?" Si didn't seem surprised.

"I don't know. Either they don't have a Wi-Fi signal this time or he's giving me the cold finger." Sam rested his elbows on his knees and hung his head.

"Not to add to your metrosexual meltdown—"

"If you're trying to insult me by implying it's better to pound your problems into the dust or ignore them for, oh, say, *ten years* I think I'll stick with talking issues through in a civilized fashion. Thank you."

"Blah, blah. But, dude, I think you meant cold shoulder. Sawyer's giving you the cold *shoulder*." Silas slapped Sam in the center of his back hard enough to make the breath wheeze from his lungs. His brother left his hand on top of the tattoo there.

"Uh, nope. Gramps." Sam angled his face so he could smirk up at Si. "He's ignoring my texts. You know, the cold finger."

"Lame," Silas groaned.

"Look who's talking, gimpy." Sam danced out of his brother's reach and leaned against the rail. Though he might have earned an ass kicking for leaving Sawyer in the dark, he didn't think he could survive one from the freaking hulk Silas had turned into. A noogie and a wedgie were one thing. He'd endured plenty of those growing up. Damage inflicted by those tree-trunk arms would be something else entirely.

"Son of a bitch." A scowl marred Silas's face when he dropped onto the stair after attempting to lurch to his feet. He looked too much like the man who'd joined their videoconferences from the emotional tundra he'd isolated himself in while living in Alaska.

"I'll take a rain check, okay?" Sam hoped Silas would forget by the time he'd healed up when he offered, "You can take a free swing once you're back to normal."

"Not necessary." Si crossed his arms over his chest. "It just sucks, you know? There's so much to do. I can't pitch in like I want. I know I say this every damn day but... Fuck. Colby crashed at the dinner table last night after covering JD's shift. I couldn't even help him to bed. Lu had to do it. Do you know how shitty it feels to watch your spouse shoulder your burdens? Both of them really. Colby wouldn't have been so fucking tired if I could have worked beside him yesterday afternoon."

First of all, Lucy was actually Colby's wife not Silas's. Technically. Sam had always known she'd belonged with both men even if his adolescent mind hadn't comprehended all the possibilities the world held. They'd seemed right together. He'd never admit it to Silas, but watching Lucy suffer after his brother's desertion had been hard for everyone left on the ranch. So much grief.

"They have you here, Silas. That's what they need most. There are plenty of hands to do grunt work. And if there's not enough labor, I can collaborate with Cindi to estimate some increases in the payroll budget and how that'll affect operating income. She's supposed to bring me the profit and loss statement sometime today so I can dig in a little deeper. We can juggle things around. Make it work without eroding margin. If not... I can cover it."

"Sure. Whatever. I don't know what the fuck you're saying, but I get the point. Still, what the hell good am I to anyone like this?" He yanked the ripped denim of his jeans, baggier over his healing thigh.

"We're stronger together." Sam gazed out at the ranch. "Which is why I should have ignored you all and called Sawyer right away. We should all be home. You're not the only one with the brand on your back, you know."

"Let me see it."

"What?" Sam glanced over his shoulder, then faced his brother once more.

"Take your shirt off."

"Kinky, Si. Shouldn't you save that for Colby?" He laughed when Silas flipped him the bird.

"Or maybe you pussied out?" Si raised an eyebrow.

"Hell, no." Sam grabbed his T-shirt and whipped it over his head. He spun on his booted heel, facing away from his brother to display the design he'd swear he'd been born with. Even when Snake had etched it into his skin, he'd imagined the artist scratched away a covering and let it shine from within, where it had always lived.

Sam opened his eyes. Which is when he saw her. Cindi. Approaching from the direction of the barn, fifteen feet away and closing fast.

"A present from your older, wiser brother. Happy early birthday." Silas flicked Sam's earlobe as he gained his feet. It stung every bit as much as it had when they were young.

Motherfucker.

"You can thank me later," Si whispered before he limped into the house.

"Wow." Cindi stood in the patchy grass at the base of the porch stairs, cradling the financial binder she'd made for Sam. She cleared her throat. "Um. Nice tattoo."

More like holy-fucking-smoking-hot man with

ripped shoulders and amazing artwork nestled between them. It had seemed organic to his body from the glimpse she'd gotten before he spun around.

Smart, sexy, sophisticated, cut *and* tattooed? She couldn't help but stare. Damn the dim barn for stealing the discovery from her two weeks ago. Her body ached for a rematch.

His T-shirt hung from his fingers and she willed him not to cover up the spectacular view. When he looked like he might, she asked, "Could I see it before you do that?"

"Hmm?" He didn't seem to understand her question.

She climbed the stairs, trailing her fingers over his shoulder to keep him still while she circled around behind him. Standing on the riser above Sam, she set the binder on the floor of the porch, then outlined the enormous compass that spanned the width of his back.

"This is gorgeous." Cindi resisted the devil on her shoulder. The corrupt bastard encouraged her to lick the swirled shading around the emblem.

"All my brothers have the same one. Got them when we turned eighteen."

"No shit." She imagined lining the four of them side by side along one of the fence rails, naked from the waist up, their tight asses highlighted by faded denim. Their bold tattoos would make a striking image, not to mention the solid men carrying them.

Despite the heat of the afternoon, she shivered.

"Only difference is the letter. Obviously, Si's N is the highlight of his." He peered over his shoulder.

Cindi couldn't help herself. She traced the ornate E on Sam's right side. "I have to admit, it makes me think better of you."

His shoulders shook beneath her light touches. "Because I'm not such a giant nerd?"

"What? No." She somehow progressed from admiring his ink to massaging his back. He didn't object so she kept kneading the solid expanse. The planes of muscle soaked up the pressure of her fingers. She traced her thumbs along either side of his spine, savoring his groan. "Because you never really abandoned your home. You knew how important this place is. How fortunate you were. Are, actually."

"Hell, yes." He turned around.

Her hands naturally rested on his shoulders, steadying them both where they perched. Eye to eye, she couldn't deny he told the truth

"I never doubted Compass Ranch was special. I wouldn't have traded it or my family for anything. But loving where you're from and aching to see the rest of the world are two different things." He shrugged, lifting her hands a bit.

She understood what he meant. When her parents were alive, she'd flown all over the globe and loved each of the distinct cultures she'd explored. Those experiences had helped her be sure this was the place meant for her.

"So you always planned to come back?" She wondered where he'd been these last two years. Other than behind a desk in Manhattan.

"I guess I didn't think that far ahead." He frowned. "No, maybe that's not true. It's more like I never imagined Compass Ranch wouldn't be waiting for me after I'd done what I needed to do, however long that took."

"I guess that's what happens when you grow up somewhere so stable." She leaned toward his strength. The idea alone attracted her like few other things could. "I'm not going to lie, Sam. I'm jealous."

His hands landed on her waist when she would have broken their contact.

"Of what, Cin?" The nickname from him sent shivers up her spine. "Is it better to understand from a young age how things really work? Or to live in blissful ignorance until your life is ripped apart and taken away forever? Maybe I haven't learned how to cope. Maybe I won't be able to handle it. You know, like when a person tries to learn a language after their formative years. Sometimes it's not possible. Sometimes losing things can fuck people up even when you were sure your bond would stay solid no matter what."

"Is that what you're scared of?" She cupped his cheeks in her palms.

"Yeah." He let her guide his head to her chest. "I'm afraid pulling JD out of the equation will be like taking the keystone from an arch and everything will tumble to the ground. What else will change? How much will survive? It's like knowing a massive earthquake is about to shake up everything I've ever known and alter the landscape forever."

"I can understand that." Since he'd broken the horrible news to her, she'd had many sleepless nights herself. "But I honestly don't think that's the case. You're going to be okay, Sam. You and your brothers will carry on. You'll uphold the traditions and values your dad instilled in you."

"So what has *you* frightened?" He must have detected her trembling.

"Losing my home." No reason to lie.

"That won't happen." Sam lifted his head and brushed his thumb over the corner of her lips. "No one's forcing you out, okay?"

"You're sure?" She swallowed hard. "I sort of thought now that you were back, you might want the cottage for yourself."

"No way." He frowned. "I'd never steal your place. JD has made it clear you're part of Compass

Ranch. The cottage is your home as much as the room upstairs is mine for now. Probably more. The baseball posters are a little outdated. And I sure could use a bigger bed."

A soft laugh puffed from her lips. Relief overwhelmed her better judgment. "So you're saying I should buy you a Playboy calendar for Christmas?"

"More like a print of Monet's *Water Lilies*." His hands surrounded her upper arms.

She could do one better than that. He wouldn't have to know the painting she gifted him with was an original. "You have good taste in art."

"I know something magnificent when I see it." He stared straight into her eyes.

How could she resist the tenderness there? Or the sizzle that sprang from the contact of their skin.

Cindi whimpered as she threaded her fingers into his still-short hair. The strands, longer now than they'd been when he arrived, teased the sensitive dips between her fingers and her palm. "Cowboy, are you going to kiss me or what?"

He ate up the sliver of space between them and pressed their lips together. His mouth curved against hers as he nuzzled her in an innocent connection. At least, that's how it started.

Their lips parted simultaneously and they sipped from each other, sampling the flavor of their partner as though their first kiss in two weeks were a naughty version of an *amuse-bouche*. After relishing the appetizer, they progressed to the entrée. Or was it straight to decadent dessert?

She nipped his bottom lip, then licked the spot she'd pinched.

His hands migrated to her ass. They slipped into her back pockets, cupping her and keeping her close while he grazed her mouth with a series of fun yet sensual kisses. Making out with Sam was like nothing she'd ever done before. He was a lip-lock connoisseur. Each touch tailored for her alone—every reaction measured and incorporated into his next approach.

Cindi let him eat at her. Instead of the overwhelming vigor of the rough and tumble cowboys she'd relied on for comfort, he concentrated on making each glide of their lips a quality encounter.

She allowed her hands to roam across his back and next to his rock-hard abs. The gym had granted him definition. She enjoyed it more than the bulk of the men who worked hard and drank harder in the bunkhouse every night. She wished she could see him, all of him, in the dazzling sunlight.

"Didn't take you long to put the moves on our little Cindi, did it, city slicker?" Jake snarled as he strolled through the yard with a half-dozen of the hands.

Engrossed in her honest exchange, Cindi hadn't heard the guys approach.

Sam bristled.

"It's not worth getting in a fight over." She dropped one last peck on his shoulder. Better to walk than face Sam's derision if Jake spilled the beans on their little game. Not to mention the world record she and Sam had set for sex on acquaintance. "I should get back to work anyway. The statements…"

He snagged the binder off the decking and thumped his hand on it. "Got them. Thanks."

His sweet tone held no malice toward her, though he glared at Jake.

She descended the stairs, making sure to hold the rail since her knees were wobbly and might stay that way for a week.

"You can be such an asshole." She slapped her palm on Jake's shoulder to squeeze past when he crowded her. He knew better than to trail her.

Sam watched Cindi retreat with a mix of regret and relief. If they hadn't been interrupted, he might have invited her inside for an iced tea or some afternoon delight in his too-short bed. While he had no doubt he would have enjoyed the hell out of her, he didn't need that kind of stress on top of everything else.

"She's a free agent. But you better limit your fucking to below the belt. Don't break her heart or screw with her head." Jake passed beyond good-natured teasing into something truly menacing. His hands balled into fists. "Or you'll find you don't have too many friends around these parts anymore."

Why did it seem like all the cowboys stared at Sam as though he'd tried to run off with their kid sister or maybe even their daughters? Hell, all he'd done was kiss Cindi. Why should he fight it when she understood him so completely? He hadn't even slipped his tongue between those supple lips.

Okay, maybe a tiny bit.

Not nearly as much as he wished he had.

"Everything all right out here?" Silas swung from the kitchen, coming to stand at the top of the stairs.

Just what Sam needed, his injured big brother to intimidate the bullies ganging up as if they'd like to flush his geeky head in a toilet. "Fine, Si. Everything's fine."

With one last look toward the barn where Cindi had disappeared, he headed inside. There was plenty for him to do now that he had data. Burying himself in figures came naturally.

Chapter Ten

Three weeks after returning to Compass Ranch

Sam peeked around the lace covering the kitchen window every time the rumble of an engine accompanied Vicky's humming.

"I haven't seen you this excited since you were a boy. Remember when JD set you up on those correspondence courses in economics?" Vicky paused sweeping the floor to kiss his cheek. "You'd pace waiting for Mr. Glenn to bring the mail."

"Please, never utter that again." He grimaced. "Was I really such a dork?"

"Nah. A serious little man, that's all. It was cute. Still is." She straightened the fabric, then whacked him in the ass with the broom. "Now keep your hands off my curtains."

He settled into his spot at the table, unable to concentrate on fund analysis or the farm's ledgers this morning. Watching Vicky complete her routine chores, it struck him how odd their life had become. Struggling for normalcy while nothing remained the same as even a month ago. JD aged about a year every day—a little more tired, a little slower. And here she was, still plugging along.

"Ma?"

"Sammy?" She winked over her shoulder, using his long-forgotten nickname.

"Are you okay?" He couldn't think of a more subtle method than to ask outright. "With all this?"

She swept the same spot in the floor about a dozen times.

Rising from the table, he encircled her in a hug. "It's all right if you're not, you know. You can talk to me. I'm here to support JD, but I'm here for you too."

"Oh, shoot." Tears pooled in her vivid eyes. "I was doing fine. You're so sweet, Sam. So different than your brothers. Not that there's anything wrong with them."

She lifted the hem of her apron to soak up the moisture leaking from her scrunched lids.

"Truth is, it's hard." She winced. "When I keep going it's bearable. If I stop to think…that's when trouble hits. It's exhausting. Thank God we have Lucy to take care of all the medicine and check-ups. I don't know how people do it when they have to go to the doctor's office day after day. I'm starting to understand why that girl carts home Christmas presents by the trunkful. She's an angel to her patients and their families. Still, how much can one person do? It's too much to ask."

Sam took the broom from her and finished building the tiny mound of dust.

"I'm here to help. We all are. Sawyer will be, too, soon." He debated contacting the Coast Guard at least a handful of times every day.

"That's the thing, Sam." A huge sigh escaped her chest. "Wishing for more time is selfish. I know it. JD is hurting. More than anything, I don't want him to suffer through a long, drawn-out affair. He's determined to see your brother's wedding. And Sawyer…"

She clung to him then, making him stumble a few tiny steps to keep his balance. Sobs ripped from her throat, terrifying him. He held her close and rocked her as she had done for him on those nights his brothers had convinced him an alien hid under his bed, lurking until dark to rip him away from his family.

Like a brutal summer storm, Vicky's grief was fierce, but rained out quickly.

"I'm sorry," she whispered.

"Nothing to apologize for. I should have asked sooner." He shook her shoulders a little. "When it starts to be too much, come find me. We'll talk. Okay?"

"Deal. But, Sammy…if you're this much better than the rest at handling your emotions…"

He separated himself and retreated a pace. "Yes?"

"Why haven't you been knocking down Cindi's door? I heard you kissed her. Is that true?"

"Jeez, Ma." He slapped his palm on his forehead. "I don't know if I did or she did or well, anyway, it was just one time."

Plus one amazing night in the barn.

And she hadn't come looking for him afterward. Probably for the best.

"From what I heard it was a really good one, though." Vicky giggled as he turned red. To see her smile, he'd have suffered the mild embarrassment a hundred times over.

"You can say that again." No sense in denying it.

"And you let her walk away? Nothing since then?" Vicky propped her hands on her hips.

"I was waiting for her to come to me." He sank into one of the dining room chairs.

"What kind of nonsense is that?" Vicky squinted

at him. "Women like to be chased."

"Well, maybe not Cindi." He shrugged. "JD told me not to scare her off."

"And you think making out with her would have her hightailing it for the hills? I'm guessing you're a better kisser than that! If not, maybe you better talk to one of your brothers. Lucy, Colby and Jody seem to have no complaints." She laughed. "Honey, your pa didn't explain himself well enough. Physical exchanges aren't going to frighten that girl one iota. It's *this* you need to worry about."

Vicky waved her hand in the space between them.

"What do you mean?" He scooted his chair closer to her.

"She spends a lot of time at the house, you know? Always has. Now every time she stops over in the evenings for dinner, or drinks after, you two end up chatting in the corner until you realize the rest of the group has wandered off. Don't think I haven't noticed. There's something there. Things drawing you together. You have loads in common. If you start to fall for her or the other way around and things hit a bump in the road. Well, I could see *that* terrifying her. In her mind, she'd be risking a lot by dating you."

"What's that supposed to mean?"

"Maybe you'd better ask her." Vicky glanced away. "I'd prefer to be direct, but I won't break her confidence. I think of her as the daughter I never had. Well, I suppose now I have two or three. What a nice benefit to you boys. Lucy has been part of our family since the first day she tagged along with her dad on a call. Cindi was the same. Popped in when her tire went flat and Jake rescued her, never did leave again. Now Jody…"

She continued to ramble, as though he could be that easily distracted.

"Ma—"

The hiss of airbrakes deploying caught his attention. He looked between Vicky and the yard. Torn.

A laugh erased the worry lines in her forehead. "Go ahead, run out and play. I'll be here later if you need some advice."

"I might just take you up on that." He hugged her one last time. "Thanks."

"Anytime, Sammy. Anytime."

He raced out the door, shutting it carefully before leaping the stairs entirely. A green car-carrier hogged most of the free space in the yard. And there, on the second level, sat his gleaming Maserati.

Sam focused on suppressing a happy dance, which would subtract at least half the cool-points he'd gained with the coupe in the first place, while the crew unloaded her. "Oh, how I missed you."

"You want it here, or in the barn?" the driver and his assistant asked while Sam signed a receipt. "Hope you're not going to leave this beauty out in the open."

"Wasn't planning on it." He thought of the space he'd cleared in the equipment storage facility. The Garage Mahal could easily accommodate a dozen extra vehicles in addition to the tractors. "But I think I might have to take her for a spin first."

That and he'd have to dig up some soft covers to keep the dust under control. He'd resigned himself to the fact that maintaining the gleaming finish he had in the city would be impossible. The promise of open road and more satisfying driving consoled him.

"Sounds like fun." The assistant said his final goodbyes to the Maserati, then climbed into the passenger seat of the rig with one last backward glance.

The truck took off slowly, but kicked up a cloud. No doubt, Sam would need those blankets. He stared at the barn for a full thirty seconds before deciding. What the hell?

He jogged to the building and swung inside.

The dim interior prevented him from noticing Cindi until he nearly plowed her over.

"Oomph." She grunted when he wrapped his arms around her to keep her from bouncing off his chest and onto her pretty ass.

"Shit. Sorry about that." He grinned. "Guess I got a little excited."

"About what? I thought I heard something." She peered around him. "Holy crap!"

"They delivered my car." He kept beaming.

"I see that." She brushed past him, intent on examining the sleek lines and gleaming paint.

"It's a—"

"Maserati Grand Turismo S." She impressed the hell out of him. "Excellence through passion and all that."

And then he did something absurd. Before he could think better of it he asked, "Know how to drive a manual transmission?"

"I hardly ever grind the gears." When he winced, she laughed. "Kidding, Sam. I've been driving stick since I turned sixteen."

He resisted the joke at least two of his brothers would have made. Seth was probably too much of a gentleman to go where Sam had in his mind.

"I've never let anyone drive her before."

"I'd settle for a ride." She smiled.

Ah, fuck it. It'd be worth a few hundred miles off the clutch to see Cindi's face light up. Her somber tone at dinners this past week had roused suspicions. His dad had flat out asked if Sam was screwing around with her. When he'd crossed his heart and said no, JD hadn't seemed much happier. A guy couldn't win sometimes. "Catch."

She snatched his keys out of the air. "Sweet!"

They tucked into the sleek interior. Cindi had to move his seat up a solid six inches and adjust the mirrors, but somehow it didn't bother him to watch her getting comfortable in his car.

"Buckle up." The wattage of her grin made up for sacrificing time behind the wheel. "I hope you don't have any objection to me obliterating the speed limit on those long, straight stretches east of here."

"I'm pretty sure Silas will bail us out if we need him to." Sam smiled. "Go for it."

She put him at ease by rolling across the yard, dodging the bigger dips that were nothing for a pickup but potentially damaging with less than five inches of clearance. When they reached the main road, she used her signal, then eased onto the blacktop.

The instant rubber settled onto the clean surface and she'd straightened out, she gunned the engine. Sam admired the quick flicks of her slender wrist and her short-shifting technique. He doubted he could have accelerated as smoothly.

Her skill turned him on.

He whooped, adjusting himself discreetly as he rolled down the window to bask in the buffeting ripples of the wind.

Content to revisit his childhood stomping grounds, Sam studied the countryside. Some things, like infinite lines of hay bales stationed at regular intervals across the Smith's spread, looked identical to his memories. Others, like old man Miller's farm, had changed completely. Instead of the simple, red-painted wood structure, a sleek, modern facility occupied the prime real estate at the intersection of two county highways.

As though she could read his thoughts, Cindi filled him in. "Mr. Miller passed away about a year ago.

His sons sold out to one of those agriculture coalitions. Impersonal, but they do have some revolutionary ideas for improving productivity we, I mean Compass Ranch, could put to good use."

"You're allowed to claim us." He smiled at her. "It takes a hell of a lot of people to make an operation as big as ours run smoothly. You play an important part."

She didn't answer him. Her concentration stayed on the road as they cracked triple digits on the speedometer while still in fourth gear.

"When you come to the juncture with 203, take it north. I want to show you something." He grinned when she accelerated through the corner and up the gentle slope of the hill. The skill she harnessed had his engine revving twice as fast as the Maserati's.

Competent, gorgeous and full of surprises. *Damn.* "Slow down."

Cindi pouted as she let off the gas.

"It'll be worth it, I promise." He couldn't help but laugh.

"Not sure that's possible."

"I'll prove it to you. Turn off here." A narrow drive led up to a gate. Sam fished a copy of the ranch's master key from his pocket. He hopped out and unlatched the padlock. A heavy chain banged against the metal post as the panel swung open.

"Where are we?" Cindi peered around the wooded path.

"You'll see in a minute. Go slow. It's paved but rocky in spots. Especially after a hard rain." He nodded when she advanced at a snail's pace. "Has it stormed a bunch this summer?"

There was a time when the weather was as important as his morning edition of *The Wall Street Journal.* Recently, it hardly mattered except for determining the view out of his sky-top office. He had migrated daily between climate-controlled environments—his apartment, his car, the garages on either end of his commute and his office.

He hated how disconnected from nature he'd become. Sam breathed deep of the crisp mountain air.

Before they'd driven more than a quarter of a mile, a wider clearing opened up. Large stones ringed the lookout.

"Oh. Wow." Cindi stopped the car and rushed toward the edge of the circle.

"Careful." Sam caught her, banding his arms around her waist from behind. "It drops off fast right on the other side of those rocks."

Pebbles bounced from their toes off the ledge, tumbling for a long while until he could no longer hear the disturbance in the brush. For long minutes they stared together at the sky, the land, and—far in the distance—the main buildings of Compass Ranch. Cindi didn't attempt to squirm from his hold. She filled his arms with warmth and softness.

He traced her gaze toward the cottage she'd claimed as her home and felt her sigh. The foreman's cabin, where Colby, Lucy and Silas lived, seemed closer when viewed from up here. Everything in sight held memories for him.

"See that ridge over there?" Sam pointed as he whispered in her ear.

She followed his finger with her wide-eyed stare.

"Mmm hmm." As though it were too much to speak, she purred her assent.

"My brothers and I used to hang out up there all the time. It was the place we spent our last night together. Silas told us he was leaving and we raced our horses up there for one final bonfire." He closed his eyes as he remembered the pain of losing his brother.

"There can be other times." Cindi spun in his arms. She rested her hands on his chest as she peered up into his eyes. "You just took a break. Soon, the four of you can enjoy each other's company again. All of you together."

"Fuck, I miss Sawyer." He clutched her tight to his chest and buried his face in her sweet smelling hair. Simple strawberry shampoo had never seemed so delicious before.

"I'm sure he would say the same." She petted his shoulders, soothing the trembling he wished he could blame on the occasional gusts of wind buffeting their hideaway and stirring the layers of her tiered sundress.

"There won't be any coming home for JD." He hated the crack in his voice.

"You can't come home to a place you've never left." Cindi drew back so he could meet her stare. Tears brimmed and overflowed, decorating her cheeks with glistening diamonds. "His spirit will always be a part of this place. Our home."

"Cin." He had to know more about her. How could she understand him so perfectly? "Where's your family?"

She squirmed free of his grasp, making him wish he'd kept his big mouth shut. She crouched, perching on one of the boulders. He dropped one hand to her shoulder, supporting her while she bent to scoop up a handful of the fine dirt at the base of the stone.

Grains of sand ran through her fingertips and spilled onto the current of air supporting three hawks as they swirled and dived through the canyons. Their cries made the only sound for long seconds. Sam resigned himself to the fact that she didn't intend to answer.

When the last granules dropped from her hand, she whispered, "Gone."

"How?" He sat beside her, entwining their

fingers.

"My mom died of breast cancer." She shook her head. "My dad couldn't stand the loss. He killed himself the same night. They didn't tell me she was sick. I was away at college. Our— Someone who worked with my father called and gave me the news."

"Jesus." He couldn't help himself. He tugged her into his lap and surrounded her with his arms, absorbing her shudders. "How could they do that? Steal those moments from you?"

She didn't respond right away. Then she cleared her throat. "If things start to go downhill faster than expected, *I'll* call Sawyer. I hope you understand."

"We'll do it together." He tucked his chin against her crown. "He should be here."

"It's just four and a half weeks right?" She hiccupped. "Surely that's not too long."

He cupped her jaw in his palm and tipped her face toward his. "JD's a stubborn old bastard. I'm sure it'll be okay."

Somehow saying it out loud made him believe it a little more.

Cindi nodded. "You've already tried to reach your brother, haven't you?"

He couldn't lie to her. "Yeah. I've called and texted him at least a dozen times and even considered sending a letter. They usually have opportunities to communicate at port. Something. I'm not sure why he hasn't responded."

"It's not your fault he's missing." She tugged him lower, then rubbed her lips across his. "You're doing what you should. Hang in a little longer."

Sam sipped from her mouth, digesting the solace she offered. He closed his eyes as he pressed their bodies together as tightly as he could, slipping his tongue inside her mouth. He traced her gums, the roof of her mouth and flicked along her similarly seeking muscle.

They groaned into each other.

When they separated, a wave of dizziness assaulted him, though not from the heights they stared out at.

Afraid of losing his balance, he tugged her backward, away from the edge. He scooped her into his arms and carried her to the car. But holding her close wasn't enough to soothe the desperation corroding his guts.

"Sam?" She mewled his name.

"Yeah, kitten?" He growled against the curve of her neck.

"You were right." She sighed. "That was *so* worth it. Better even than the view from the Eiffel Tower."

"The one in Vegas?" He nodded. "The lights on the strip are impressive, and it's an awesome place to watch the Bellagio fountains across the street."

"True, but I meant the real one. In Paris."

"Right." Why had he assumed she'd never traveled abroad? Maybe she'd taken a class trip in high school or a once in a lifetime jaunt with some friends.

"I'd say it even beats the cable car from Montjuïc in Barcelona or the Sydney Harbor Bridge climb or the observation deck on the Petronas Twin Towers in Kuala Lumpur." She grinned up at him. "None of those places meant as much to me as Compass Ranch. And I never shared the view with a man like you."

Christ, he'd agree with her on Paris, Montjuïc and Sydney but he wouldn't know about Kuala Lumpur since he'd never been there. "How have you gone so many places?"

She shrugged. "Does it matter? This is the one I love most."

The power of her conviction, and the one little L word nestled in the middle, hit him in the gut. What would he do for a woman who aimed that passion at him instead of his home? A hell of a lot. "Why didn't you come see me after...?"

"The day we kissed on the porch?" She cocked her head at him.

"Yeah. I mean, you've been up to the house for dinner, sure. But we never really discussed that day. Or the night in the barn."

"I figured you had enough on your mind without complicating things." She rested her head on his shoulder as he approached the car.

"Maybe I like obstacles."

"Maybe you don't understand all the issues at play." She worried her lip between her teeth.

"Tell me what you're hiding." He set her on the hood of his car, not giving a fuck about his precious paint job. "We can work through it together."

"I can't," she whispered. "You'd never understand. I have certain...needs."

"Share and I'll do my best to satisfy them." He'd never craved being what someone wanted so badly.

"Not possible." She hung her head. "Even now, with you here, I'm thinking of...other things. It's not fair."

"Let me take your mind off everything but me." He ran his hand up her thigh, inching her skirt higher and higher.

"You can try," she whispered.

If he'd ever heard a challenge so sweet he couldn't remember it.

He thought his dick had taken extra notice when his pants buzzed. Until it happened again and again in rapid succession. Damn, cell phone on vibrate. With a curse, he jammed his hand in his pocket and hit the silence button, then threw the device through the open car door.

"You should get that." Cindi glanced back and forth between him and the front seat.

"Is that really what you want me to do right now?" He kept one hand on her waist, steadying her on the inclined metal surface.

"Hell, no."

"That's what I thought." Sam stepped between her spread knees, buried his fingers in her hair and kissed the shit out of her. He prodded the delicate straps from her shoulders and peeled the fitted bodice of her dress off her voluptuous breasts, prettier than he remembered.

He set a world record for unhooking a strapless bra with one hand while he entertained her with a series of sultry kisses over her mouth, neck and collarbones. By the time he reached her chest, he'd bared the creamy skin there to the glorious sun and his hungry, questing lips.

She arched into his hold, nudging one nipple into his mouth. He accommodated her request by suckling slow and light at first, building to a hard, quick flutter of pressure.

"Yes!" she shouted into the expanse of nature surrounding them, cocooning them in the blissful peace of the spot and their shared timeout from reality. "More, please."

"Happy to oblige, ma'am." He relished the rumble of her chuckle through her breastbone as he slid his lips across to the matching mound on the opposite side of her chest. The light, salty zest of her skin tasted like perfection to him. Better than a million gourmet meals.

Still, other delicacies appealed to his appetite.

He pressed her shoulders with one hand and

caught her with the other until she steadied on her palms, braced behind her ass. "Okay, kitten?"

"Hell no."

He paused in his descent, keeping his grip on her waist.

"No, no." She laughed, using one hand to muss his hair. "Keep going. Faster."

Sam grinned as he spread her thighs wider. Pretty floral panties were revealed to his seeking gaze. He nuzzled the damp spot between her legs, breathing deep. She smelled better than the roses on the fabric would have.

He nipped the inside of her thigh. When she squealed, he soothed the spot with long laps of his tongue. Then he previewed his skills by tracing intricate patterns over the inflamed flesh. Just as he'd torture her clit in a minute.

Cindi wriggled, inspiring him to tighten his fingers on her hips to prevent her from sliding off his car, which had never looked as sexy as it did with its seductive new hood ornament. Sam spared one hand to whip the thin cotton from her, tossing it over his shoulder.

"Hey, I like those." Her laughter took the sting from her objection.

"I'll buy you new ones. Expensive silk from China. Handmade."

"Seems like a lot of effort for undies." She kept chuckling, though moans interspersed her mirth.

"You're worth the best." He paused to meet her gaze, hoping she realized he wasn't toying with her. Every time they touched, this connection burned brighter. Fused them tighter. No matter how hard he concentrated on avoiding her, he simply couldn't. Why resist nature?

He cupped her ass and tugged her closer to his

salivating mouth. Before their flesh met, he blew on her sensitive, swollen pussy. When she twitched, he smirked. Oh yeah, this was going to be fun.

She kicked off her sandals and propped her feet on his shoulders. His hands ran from her thighs to her knees, as far as he could reach, before making the return journey. So pale and creamy, her skin begged for him to sample the peaches and cream complexion.

He taunted her, nibbling a path across the top of her close-shaved mound, then her inner thigh before skipping to the main attraction. Even then, he used only the very tip of his tongue to stimulate her moist lips, parting them to nudge at her swollen clit.

"Ah. Yes." She buried her fingers in his hair and lost her inhibitions. He could easily have resisted her tiny tug. Why bother when he craved her flavor as much as she wished to share it with him?

His lips spread as he kissed her pussy. The unique aroma of her, which he'd sworn he'd caught whiffs of on himself even days after their rendezvous in the barn, returned full force. He groaned and buried his face in the succulent treat she offered, arching her hips to grant him more thorough access.

"Oh my God." Her fingernails dug into his scalp, spurring him to devour her. "You're really good at that."

He angled his head to the side long enough to murmur, "Thanks."

His chuckle must have vibrated her pussy. She groaned and clung as he took her for a more thrilling ride, this time *on* the Maserati. He'd never look at the vehicle the same way again. Surely, its value had doubled in the last five minutes.

Sam took his time introducing her to a number of skills from his very large bag of tricks. He tried to keep her on the edge as long as possible, but somewhere between the flicky-thing mixed with the sucky-thing topped with a swirl, she completely lost it. He drank from her clenching pussy, only sorry he hadn't drawn out the pleasure for her.

Until the spasms rejuvenated around his tongue.

Multi-orgasmic too? Jesus. She couldn't get hotter if she were fucking him on the surface of the sun. He soothed her with tender licks while he prodded at her slick opening with his fingers.

"More, Cin?" He paused, waiting for her approval. He shouldn't have doubted her.

"Please. Yes." She rocked her pelvis, inserting him to his second knuckle in the saturated tissues, which still clenched rhythmically around his digits. Her toes curled into his shoulders, making him wish he could see what her pretty-painted nails looked like against the rich blue of his shirt.

Still, he didn't care enough to move. Not enough to stop finger fucking her while wringing climax after climax from her petite frame. Endless, gorgeous, wild—her passion awed him. The uninhibited display made him realize their night in the barn had been far from ideal for either of them. Holy fuck, what could it be like if they surrendered free of the emotional highs and lows that had battered them? With concentration undivided, he could make her soar.

Sam nipped her clit lightly between his teeth, leaving her sobbing in another release. This time, her entire body went slack. He had to act fast to catch her as she slumped, her dress falling neatly into place as if she hadn't just ridden his face like a champion rodeo star.

"Oh." She tried to push from his hold. Her noodle arms bounced off his chest. "My. God."

He laughed, from deep behind his diaphragm, maybe for the first time in months. Tendrils of her hair curled in the perspiration dotting her forehead. Adorable ringlets, one of them a lovely shade of lilac, made her look far more innocent than the womanly response of her body had.

"I could say the same." Sam lowered his head. Some women would balk at tasting themselves on his lips. Not Cindi.

She closed the gap and attacked his mouth, rewarding him for a job well done.

As much as he wished he could play the steadfast gentleman, he needed more. His cock might riot in his jeans if he didn't let it loose and bury it in the slick heat she generated.

"Do you have any condoms with you, kitten?"

"Damn it, no." She frowned. "I didn't expect to be leaving the barn when I ran into you. Certainly not for this. I left my purse on my desk."

"Shit." He debated the merits of protection, something he'd never done before. Finally, better sense kicked in. "No, no. That's good. Perfect. I want to make love to you in a real bed. Take our time. Go slow and easy in the gold beams of the late afternoon sunshine. Will you have me like that, Cindi?"

He crowded her, hoping she wouldn't be able to resist although he'd alleviated some of her desire.

She placed her hands on his cheeks, gently. When her lips lingered a hairsbreadth from his, she whispered, "Yes."

147

Chapter Eleven

Cindi couldn't believe she'd invited Sam to her home. Because, really, that was the only place they could possibly find some solitary space for uninterrupted loving. Even more, it shocked her to the core that the idea didn't terrify her. For the first time in years, she'd met a man she actually trusted enough to let inside, to share her secrets.

If he asked again, she'd spill her guts. He would understand. Hell, it might even turn him on. And the other stuff… Well, he had nothing to gain from her in that respect.

Maybe he read her absolute confidence in her unblinking stare because he shared something disturbing of his own. She saw it coming a mile away as he wrung the hem of her dress between his amazingly skilled fingers. Dread coalesced in her stomach.

"Cindi, I need to tell you something." He sighed. "Except now, after that, it's going to make me sound like a creeper no matter how I put it. I should have said this before we…"

"Oh boy, this sounds like fun." She wiggled her

perfectly arched brows.

His laugh had a healthy groan mixed in.

"Just spit it out, Sam." She patted his cheek, then separated them. Though she missed the steel band of his arms around her shoulders, she figured it best to find her balance. Just in case. It wouldn't be the first time life had ripped her feet out from under her. "I'm tough. I can take it."

"Okay, fine." He turned toward her, serious. "JD is taking advantage of you. You should demand a raise."

Cindi grabbed her stomach and doubled over as though she'd taken a punch to the gut. Her shoulders shook violently.

"Oh, shit." Sam rubbed her back. His hand spanned most of the width of her shoulders on each pass. "I didn't mean to upset you. I just… I saw what he's paying you when I reviewed the records. It's bullshit. You make less than some of the ranch hands, and you're skilled. Educated."

When she levered upright, he must have realized she wasn't crying. Actually, she was, but the tears squeezing from her eyes were borne of laughter.

"What the fuck is so funny about that?" He glowered as his lips thinned. "I don't like ratting out my dad."

"Oh, Sam." She closed the gap between them and hugged him tight. "I think you're right."

"Damn straight, I am. It's highway robbery."

"No, no." She could have kissed him for another decade straight. So sweet. "Not about that. We should go back to my place and talk. There's so much I'd like to share. It'll all make sense then."

"Uh, okay." He shook his head, then blinked. Several times. "I'll never understand women. Just once I'd like to have a fucking clue. I debated for a week how to break the news to you."

"You sure as hell have a firm grasp on the important concepts." Her body still hummed. God, sex with Sam alone was almost as good as playing with Jake and the rest of the cowboys. What would it be like if Sam joined them?

She shuddered.

Greedy.

Unfaithful.

If they continued down this path, she couldn't justify her affairs. At some point, she'd owe it to him to be exclusive. Some of her excitement vanished. She had to come clean. At least she had the ride home to organize her thoughts and decide on the right approach.

"Mind driving?" She smiled up at him. "I'm tuckered out."

"You're welcome." How could one man so effectively mix ego with magnetism?

He handed her into the passenger seat before jogging around to the driver's side. His heated gaze never once left hers through the windshield.

Sam dropped behind the wheel, then lifted up immediately. "What the fuck?"

He withdrew his phone from beneath his fine ass.

"Oh, shit." He glanced at the screen, his face losing all its color.

"What is it?" She placed her palm over his free hand on the gearshift. He shook it off.

"Sawyer. He tried to call." Sam swiped his finger over his Smartphone, then punched a particular spot hard enough she feared he might crack the screen. Speakerphone kicked in and a sexy, laughing voice filtered through the device.

"Hey, bro. Thought I'd let you know I had a little oopsy with my phone. Dropped the fucker overboard while I was saying goodbye to an unbelievably hot crewmate during the last supply stop. What can I say? The price was well worth it. Anyway, gotta run, only had a minute on shore this time. Wanted to check in. Had this feeling… Anyway, I hope all is well and that you're sitting in your new, shiny VP chair making millions by the fucking second. This assignment is everything I hoped and more. Can't wait to get back on the ocean again. I've been thinking more about re-upping and gotta say, this run isn't helping make the choice any easier. Or maybe it is. Talk to you soon. Don't behave!"

"Shit, shit, shit!" Sam pounded the steering wheel with each curse.

Cindi unwrapped his fist from his phone before he crushed the innocent device. "Why don't you try to redial quick? It hasn't been that long…"

"Most of an hour." He shook his head. "He's gone. I don't need technology to know it."

"Does that twin thing happen often?" She tilted her head.

"Enough." He gritted his teeth. "I can't believe I missed him because I was fucking around."

She flinched.

"Son of a bitch. I'm sorry, Cin." He scrubbed his hands over his face. "I didn't mean that."

She stared out the side window, refusing to meet his stare. Great. Just fucking terrific. Maybe she should thank him. She'd almost made an enormous mistake. Before he could patch up the craters his half-cocked mouth had made in her confidence, his phone buzzed again.

He snatched it from Cindi and punched the talk button. "Saw?"

"No." The curt response came from one of his brothers, just not the one he'd probably hoped for. "Where the hell are you? I've been trying to call you for half an hour."

"I'm…" He peeked over at Cindi, seeming to note her slumped shoulders. "Up at the lookout."

"You're chasing ass when we need you here?" The growl on the other end of the line adopted a nasty edge.

"What's up, Silas?" Sam surprised her when he didn't bother to play coy. Apparently, hearing the same crap he'd spouted not long ago from someone else seemed to jumpstart his instinctive defenses.

Maybe it hadn't been meaningless. Could the exchange have rocked him to the core, too?

"It's JD. He, fuck, I don't understand exactly." Several heavy pants filled the echoing silence on the line. "We headed home for our afternoon break but before we got there he had trouble breathing. Sweat was pouring off of him and he kept clutching at his chest. Jesus."

If she believed ranch legends, nothing scared Silas. Ever. Right now he sounded like he might shit his pants. That was enough to have ice water replacing the steam in Cindi's veins. Sam's too if his wide eyes were any indication.

"We're at the hospital. You better come quick." Silas kept talking but Sam already thrust the car into gear. He tossed the phone to Cindi and buckled up. "Find out more. Please."

She mirrored him. "Silas? Si? Oh, Lucy, thank God. This is Cindi. What's happening?"

Sam didn't wait for medical jargon to pour over them. He peeled out of the narrow drive without relocking the gate and floored the gas. They fishtailed on the pea gravel before zooming down the hills toward the nearest civilization.

"Tell them we'll be there in fifteen minutes," he rumbled at her.

When Cindi relayed the message, Lucy objected. "It's a half hour at least from the lookout to the hospital."

"If Compton Pass's sheriff has a problem with me, he can damn well try to keep up." Sam kept true to his word, flying through the countryside. His agile, focused driving didn't frighten her one bit.

The news from Lucy did.

"A pulmonary embolism?" Cindi tried to look at Sam but she couldn't see through the sheen of tears in her eyes. "That's a blood clot right? Is he..."

"They think we caught it in time. I injected him with heparin. An anticoagulant." Lucy sniffled. "It looked bad. I'm not going to lie. Just get here safe, please. We'll be waiting."

She clicked the phone off and concentrated on the man beside her.

"It's going to be okay, Sam." She rubbed his knee. "You heard Lucy. They think he'll pull through."

"This time." His solemn eyes cut to her across the intimate cabin. "Now. Later. Sometime soon. That won't be true. One of these calls will be it."

"Sam." She swallowed her agony.

"How will we handle it when it's time? How will we forge ahead when he's not going to be okay?"

She didn't have an answer for him.

Instead, she offered her hand.

He took it.

"I'm not ready to let go, Cin."

"Me either."

"That's enough, young lady." JD's stern directive greeted them as they rushed along the hall, no need to check in with the nurse's station for which way to turn. "Are you listening to me? Put the instruments down. Now. Go work on someone who can use your help."

Sam and Cindi ran, hand in hand. They careened around the corner. Sam almost crashed into a cart of supplies outside a pale green room. A harried nurse fled the scene, blazing past them in her orthopedic sneakers.

He jammed into the crowded room, tugging Cindi after him. Silas, Colby, Lucy, Seth, Jody, Vicki, Sam and Cindi piled the room full of tension, pride and determination. All of them together were no match for the patriarch of their family.

"Never again, you hear me. Enough hospitals. Enough doctors. Enough wasting my time. There's no point to any of this. It's gonna happen sooner or later. Probably sooner." JD met each of their stares as his gaze ringed the room. "None of you *need* me. Not even you, V. You've got each other. That's enough."

He lingered on Cindi and Sam, nodding when he spied their clasped hands.

"Well, you'd better at least wait for my wedding before kicking the bucket," Seth snarled at their dad, making the badass laugh until he coughed. "If you disappoint Jody, I'll be pissed."

"So noted." JD reached out for Seth's hand. "You have to know, all of you, that even if my winkled old ass isn't around, I'm still there for you. I've given you all everything I have. I hope that means you'll carry some part of me with you. Now, enough of this mushy shit. Take me home. I want my saggy mattress and my lumpy pillow instead of this newfangled piece of gadgetry. How can a man sleep in a rocket ship like this?"

It took several hours more to clear paperwork and sign releases. Sam figured JD held up well enough when he grumbled and bitched throughout the entire ordeal, though he allowed them to wheel him out to the car without pitching a fit. By the time they rolled into the lot, well past dark, Sam felt like he'd taken a baseball bat to the back of his skull.

And Cindi.

Shit.

She hunkered, half-asleep, against the door of his car. During the interminable wait, she'd fetched coffee, held hands, doled out hugs and lent her ear, even to his beastly brothers. Not for one moment did she feel like a stranger. Hell, she meshed better with them than he did most of the time.

And that's when he'd realized the truth. He couldn't afford to fuck this up by rushing into something he didn't have the heart to pursue with every fiber of his being. Not now. He'd tried the distracted love affair thing with Belinda, and look how that'd turned out.

They climbed from the car as though the effort required was equal to jogging up ten flights of stairs.

"Just say it, Sam." She sighed. "Fast and painless."

"I feel like I owe you better than half my attention." He shook his head, grimacing. "The timing. It's bad. Awful."

"I understand." She lifted onto her tiptoes to kiss his cheek.

It didn't help his conscience that she seemed completely sincere.

"It's too much all at once." Her fingers lingered on his hand, falling slowly as she stepped away. "Go on inside. With your family. I'm heading home."

"Are you sure you'll be all right by yourself?" Sam couldn't find a way to show her that he considered her part of their Compass Ranch clan too. She shouldn't have to be isolated with this kind of agony. But how could he keep her close and not want...more? "You shouldn't be alone. Would you rather stay in Si's old room?"

"Nah. I bet Colby, Lucy and Si will camp out there." She took a step backward. "I'll be fine. Don't want to get under anyone's feet. Or be in the way."

"You wouldn't..."

"Sam?" Vicky poked her head out the screen door. "Oh, Cin. I didn't realize you were still here."

"Just leaving." Cindi trudged up the stairs and hugged Vicki before whispering something in her ear.

His mom murmured in return. Sam, still frozen in the spot where Cindi had left him standing, couldn't hear the exchange. Cindi shook her head, then scurried across the yard to her truck before he could snag her wrist and beg her not to leave him after all.

She waved at them before creeping out of the drive in a cloud of dust.

"Sorry, Sammy."

"Not your fault, Ma." He rubbed his nape but the tension there didn't subside. "I can't seem to figure out the right thing with her."

"What's your heart telling you?" She smiled at him.

"That I screwed up." He shook his head. "I shouldn't have let her go. But now it's too late."

"It's never too late, honey." Vicky patted his chest. "Grab some extra blankets from the storage shed, please. There's a green tote with a bunch of clean linens. We're going to need them with this full house. Once you haul them in here, I won't mind if you disappear for a bit."

She grinned, and he answered with one of his own.

But after he'd collected the supplies and passed them out, he could hardly keep his eyes open. He crashed on the couch in his office and rested them...just for a minute. And after he woke, several hours later, neck stiff from the awkward angle he'd stuck it in on the battered furniture, he felt like the moment had passed. Cindi had slipped through his fingers again.

Grief left him short on motivation and hope.

It might be best to let her escape their turmoil for now.

No need to infect others with his misery more than he already had.

"Sleep well, Cindi." He stared out the windows in the direction of her cottage as he drifted off once more.

Chapter Twelve

Five weeks after returning to Compass Ranch

Three bangs on the half-open door to the screened porch where Sam had set up his temporary office startled him as he was about to initiate a strategic trade. His hand lurched from the mouse and grabbed his chest.

Silas, Colby and Seth raided his sanctum.

"What the fuck was that for?" He glanced back at his screen, watching the ticker scroll a new—higher—cost for the cornerstone stock he'd almost snagged at bargain-basement prices. "Shit!"

"Enough of this." Silas pressed the screen of his laptop closed while Seth spun his desk chair around.

"You just cost me several grand, Si." He would have tugged his hair if it had been long enough. Hell, soon it would be. It'd been over a month since he'd had it trimmed to its usual shortness.

"Don't worry, we'll all be taking a share of your cash before the night is through." Colby knocked his boot into Sam's bare foot. "Get fucking dressed. Enough of this moping around."

"Who's moping? I'm *working*." Sam's blood

boiled. "Just because I'm not out there swinging a shovel—"

"Hey now, no one's disagreeing about that." Colby intervened before things could disintegrate into a legendary Compass Brother fistfight. "But enough is enough."

"You're not going to spend every minute of every day buried in this fucking thing or running to help JD every time he wheezes." Silas gestured toward the laptop. "There's still a world outside this freaking sunroom and his sickroom, you know?"

Sam stretched. He *was* starting to feel like he'd been molded into the shape of this goddamned chair and he couldn't remember the last time he'd changed his T-shirt. He grinned. "All right. What'd you have in mind?"

"Poker night." Seth put his hand out and Sam took it. His brother hauled him to his feet.

"Cards, alcohol for the rest of you and trash talk." Si grinned. "What more could a man ask for?"

The glance Silas and Colby shared was so full of dirty intentions Sam had to look away.

"Does it make you uncomfortable?" Colby put his hand on Sam's shoulder.

"Only if jealous counts." Sam brushed past them, ignoring the ache in his heart, which hadn't quite healed. Surrounded by his brothers and their fan-fucking-tastic partners, was it any wonder he'd buried his nose in business?

"She wasn't good enough for you, Sam." Seth followed as he clomped up the stairs.

"Who?" He glanced over his shoulder.

"The bitch in New York. I'm not stupid, you know?"

"I know. About both you and Belinda." He really did. Still, he ached for someone who understood.

159

Someone like Cindi, the woman he'd shoved off.

In the five weeks since he'd been home, JD had declined in fits and starts. Sure, there were good days. The bad ones scared the shit out him. His dad never seemed to recover all the way after one of those and a significant amount of ground had been lost.

Between anger, terror and denial, it would have been nice to have someone to hold and love to neutralize the acid burning a hole in his heart. His brothers' partners did that for them. Cindi could do the same for him. Somehow, it didn't seem fair to use her like that. If he started something, it should be for the proper reasons. Right now, he couldn't be sure his intentions were honorable. "I'll be there in fifteen. Want a shower too."

"Deal. You reek worse than the old outhouse from downwind." Seth held his nose, then left Sam alone.

Cindi laughed when Lucy and Jody fussed over her hair. If they pouffed it any bigger she might topple over. As it was, she feared she might look like a crazy dandelion. "Okay, okay, enough."

The women admired their handiwork.

"You're right. It's perfect." Jody pinched Cindi's ass. "You're so fucking hot in those dukes I might do you myself. Jake won't know what hit him tonight."

"I could say the same for your guys." Cindi scanned over the blonde and brunette bombshells, wishing it were a Compass Brother who'd benefit from her primping as well. Dreams of Sam plagued her daily. Okay, hourly.

She'd settle for the comfort her cowboys would gladly lavish. It wouldn't surprise her if she ended up imagining Sam in their place when they helped her chase off the ghosts of her loneliness and eliminate the artifacts of the stress dogging them all. The same thing had happened the handful of times she'd surrendered to them since Sam had put their budding affair on hold. Suddenly, the community touch had lost some of its effectiveness.

Damn Sam.

Lucy's tied, white-cotton shirt displayed a killer rack and Jody's ultra-mini denim skirt would drive her fiancé insane with glimpses of her toned derrière. Their men wouldn't hesitate to pounce on the blatant offerings. "Lucky bitches."

"Hopefully we'll all be getting lucky shortly." Lucy did a silly two-step.

"Probably need to get the show on the road. Want to bust this party up before they're too drunk to deliver." Jody wiggled her eyebrows.

The three of them strutted down the stairs of the main house and found Vicky and JD sitting at the kitchen table, sharing a late night cup of tea. It had helped JD sleep lately. As much as he could.

"Oh, if that doesn't look like a bundle of trouble, I don't know what does." JD grinned from ear to ear. "My poor boys. Have mercy, ladies."

Vicky chuckled. "Better yet, don't."

Cindi leaned in and kissed JD's cheek. It was one thing for Lucy and Jody to screw around with Seth, Silas and Colby. After all, they were married...sort of. Or almost.

"Jake won't know what hit him tonight, sweetie." He patted her hand.

"Thanks." She blushed. Did everyone know about her liaisons with the cowboy and...the rest? It wasn't like there was a love match between her and Jake but damn he could show her a good time. And he always settled her in his arms, in their mutual respect and in their shared passion for the place they'd made their home.

"If you're looking for something more…" He glanced to Vicky, who nodded. "Why not give Sam a run for his money? I've noticed him watching you. You have a lot in common, you know."

Cindi choked. "Uh, I… No, I couldn't."

Talking about JD's son had her itching to bolt. The sparks showering them every time Sam looked in her direction, despite his hands-off mandate, were freaky enough. They could talk for hours on the porch. Often did. The moment things turned hot, he'd pack up or find some excuse to disappear.

"Then I hope that boy's paying attention. His head has been so far up his ass since he got here, I swear." He frowned. "I'm gonna have to chat with him tomorrow."

Ouch. Cindi had received JD's *talks* a time or two herself. Poor Sam.

"Quit hogging the pretty ladies, JD," Vicky clucked at him. "Let them have their fun."

"You know I'm a sucker for a gorgeous woman." The heat in his stare singed Cindi, and she wasn't even the recipient. She melted inside. What would it be like to have someone love her like that—all consuming, pure and eternally?

"Be careful, sweetheart." Vicky smiled at her. "Don't settle."

Cindi might have backed out of their adventure after that except Lucy grabbed one of her elbows and Jody ensnared the other. Together, they hauled her toward the door. "Goodnight, Vicky. 'Night, JD."

"I'm guessing it will be." JD laughed as they shut the screen door carefully behind them.

The women giggled on the short journey across the yard to the barn, where the lights were blazing through the gaps around the door.

"You know, Sam is smokin'. He's suave, into fancy stuff like you and still approachable. Doesn't flaunt his brains. Could give Seth a lesson or five thousand on dealing with emotional shit. And damn that sleek bod. Do you think he was a swimmer? Anyway, maybe JD's on to something there." Jody poked her in the ribs. "I'd do him if I were you."

"Me too." Lucy licked her lips. "Nothing better than prime, grade A Compton beef."

Too late, ladies. I've already done him. And damn, he's delicious. She was ready for a second serving. Or maybe fifths.

"Plus you two get along really well. Don't think we haven't noticed how much time you spend laughing and flirting." Jody groaned. "Please, I took that route with Seth for years. Do yourselves a favor and skip to the hot stuff. You can chat in bed after he gives you a couple dozen orgasms in a row."

Lucy and Jody giggled and hugged.

Cindi's cheeks heated. *What the hell?* It's not like she was shy. Before she could fill them in on her failed attempts at seduction, they hauled open the door and marched inside the barn.

At least ten cowboys looked up from the ring of hay bales they perched on. Several whistled and cheered. Lucy strode to her men. She bent over to kiss Colby on the cheek, presenting her ass conveniently in Silas's line of sight.

"This is a guys-only event, doll," Silas rumbled before swatting the tight globes in front of him.

"Oh, really? Who's going to kick us out?" Jody slipped onto Seth's lap, crossing her legs provocatively.

"They can stay." One of the hands slurred his opinion.

"Yeah, come on over and keep me warm, honey." Duke grabbed for Cindi's wrist but she dodged.

With JD's all-knowing stare fresh in her memory, she peered between Jake and Sam. They sat side by side. She headed in their direction. An open bottle of Jack perched between them. She accosted the whiskey and took a long swig. Though she indulged in an occasional glass of wine with dinner, it had been a while since she'd hit hard alcohol.

The rush went straight to her head.

Or maybe those tingles came from Sam, who stared at the flex of her throat as she swallowed and swallowed again. She didn't quite catch every drop of the amber liquid. A trickle rolled down her chin.

"Wouldn't want to let that go to waste." Jake grinned, then tugged her toward him.

She smiled at his familiar open arms, waiting for them to enfold her in his strength. Before they could, the barn spun around her.

Sam answered with a snarl, "Certainly wouldn't."

She worried about the likelihood of a cowboy brawl as he knocked her off balance, catching her on his lap. He kissed a path from her chin to her lips, sharing the flavor of him, a hundred times more potent than any alcohol. God she'd missed that.

She blinked up into his gorgeous eyes.

"Well, I suppose if you're not gonna play cards, city slicker, I'll have to divest you of your stakes." Jake knocked a fist into Sam's knee. "Either way I win."

Cindi peeled her stare from Sam to take in the lay of the land.

The guys had been at it long enough several of them had fallen out of the running and were simply along for the ride. They added to the growing pile of beer cans, bragged about women or horses and watched the remaining players with mild interest.

In fact, only Jake and Sam had chips left in front of them.

"Don't be ridiculous." Sam tightened one arm around her waist when she would have shifted. "Now that I have a good luck charm, you're doomed."

"Hmm, seems like cheating to me." Jake rubbed his hand over her shin where it dangled closest to him. Sandwiched between them, stealing heat from both men, had her tummy doing cartwheels. "Maybe she should be part of the pot."

A bunch of the cowboys laughed or nodded in agreement.

"Hey now." Sam started to object on her behalf.

While she appreciated the sentiment, she couldn't possibly expect him to understand Jake's claim despite the knowledge most of the men in the room had. Last thing she wanted was his misplaced righteous indignation landing him in the middle of a pack of rowdy, bored, drunk cowboys. Usually that was her spot, except it wasn't fists they aimed at her.

"How good are you at cards?" She winked up at Sam.

"Poker is all about math. Odds." He grinned, then dropped a kiss on her nose. "Betting is what I do for a living, remember?"

She patted his cheek, then squirmed off his lap. "Good enough. Let the games begin."

Silas, Colby and Seth seemed to relax as she diffused the tension, taking a spot between the mounds of chips and swaying to the music that poured from the stereo they'd borrowed from her office. Lucy and Jody joined her in the center of the ring, dancing for their men and sharing the benefit with the guys who whistled and cheered for their show.

Someone passed Lucy another bottle and she took a swig before handing it to Cindi. Somehow, being the center of such obvious attention, yet not having the pressure of hands, mouths or cocks on her skin to

165

soothe the riot the men ignited in her system, unnerved her. She slugged a few shots of the potent liquid she couldn't taste beyond the fire in her esophagus, then offered it to Jody.

"Oh no, none of that for you." Seth laughed as he filched the alcohol from his fiancée before she could do some damage. "Remember last time?"

"Party pooper." Jody giggled, then ground her pelvis in seductive payback.

"Damn." Silas groaned as he observed the three women gyrating, back-to-back, for their viewing pleasure. "I think you guys better make this an all-in round. Or we're gonna start losing ranch hands to spontaneous combustion."

Sam shook his head. "Not an ideal strategy…"

"Chickenshit?" Jake's belly laugh held a sloppy note. Cindi hadn't noticed it right away. He never played with her after too much to drink. A beer or two was one thing. On occasion he took things beyond toasty to all-out hammered. It wasn't his most attractive quality.

She trusted him, though. Enough, that should he win, she had no qualms about backing out. He wouldn't hold her to this silly pissing contest. Hurting her had never been his thing. Rubbing victory in Sam's face would satisfy him. Plus, it's not like he couldn't have her any night if he asked. If he needed her like she'd needed him lately, she would take care of him.

Since Sam had put the brakes on the natural development of their relationship, the loneliness had grown to an almost intolerable ache in her gut. Sure, she'd had dinner at the main house, enjoyed girly stuff with Lucy and Jody as they worked on the wedding plans, hung out with Sam and Silas when they needed a break during the day, helped with JD and stayed when she and Sam more often than not fell into a deep conversation. But every one of those encounters only made it harder to walk away again.

For the first time in forever, Cindi wanted one man.

Who didn't want her.

Jake had been there to remind her she belonged. Could he hold some of that pain against Sam? She'd have to talk to him.

Tomorrow.

When they had clear minds.

As for tonight… She held her hand out until someone placed another bottle in it, then drank as much as she could stand. Please, God, let Sam win. Let him claim his prize. She couldn't endure this torture of wanting and not having, knowing they were perfect for each other.

Almost.

If only he didn't object to her secrets. Of course, he'd have to let her share them in order to find out once and for all. She'd settle for coming apart in his arms again. Or better yet, repaying the generosity he'd shown her the afternoon he'd taken her to the lookout.

Cindi didn't realize she'd elevated her dancing to fresh, naughty places until more whistles cut through the buzz she boosted with another couple of swallows of something that would probably be nasty if she had any taste buds left.

Sam happened to glance up just as she drew the tip of one finger from her mouth, down her neck, across the swell of her breast and rubbed her hard nipple.

"Jesus. Keep that up and I'll lose for sure." He shook his head. "Stop distracting me. I'll take two cards."

The dealer passed them to Sam. He bit his lip as he flipped them over. Could she really affect his concentration? After weeks of solid friendship, she had her doubts.

"Sexy, Cin." Jake rubbed his chest, one of his most erogenous zones. She loved to bite him there. "I'm staying where I am."

His Cheshire grin didn't do much for his poker face. He must have one hell of a hand.

She pouted but kept dancing. If nothing else, maybe she could make Sam hungry.

Jake flipped up the edge of her skirt, flashing her lacy white panties. "Very nice, Cin. I'll enjoy working them off you with my teeth."

He fanned his cards out, face up. Two pair.

Cheers and clapping met his strong showing.

"Well, shit." Sam studied the hand.

"Better luck next time, kid." Jake lurched from the hay bale and staggered toward her.

"Oh, no, my luck is fine." Sam smirked. "Just hate to see a man lose with such a fine hand."

He brandished his full house with a flourish of his wrist, splaying the cards so everyone could read them and weep.

"Nice one, bro," Silas hollered as the cowboys roared and clapped for Sam or groaned for Jake.

Cindi snagged a soft lead rope off a peg on the wall nearby, then slung it loosely around Sam's shoulders, using it to tug him to his feet. She danced for him, empowered in the place she often came to share and be shared. The steady burn of the alcohol she'd chugged didn't hurt either.

He laughed as she shimmied before him, grinding against the bulge in his jeans that proved he wasn't immune to her display. Thank God.

As she pranced out of the barn with him in tow, pausing from time to time to make a grand exit, she hoped he wouldn't let her fall flat on her face. When she peeked over her shoulder, she saw Jody doing the same to Seth and Lucy with her men. The women encouraged the guys to leave the party a little early. Their rewards would be well worth it.

Cindi aimed Sam for the back door, knowing exactly where she'd like to seduce him.

"Kitten, do you have any idea how jealous those guys are of me right now?" He groaned when she continued her sultry swaying despite having left prying eyes behind.

"All that matters to me is how you feel about it." She wished she could take another fortifying drink. Instead, she spun around, facing him as she continued to dance backward. Almost there. Twenty more feet at most, and they'd be behind the shelter of the small shed that held overflow feed and other supplies.

"Fun, Cin." His eyes were bright and his smile wide as she slowed down. "I love this side of you. Playful, casual, hot—I don't know that I've seen it before now. It balances out your sexy sophisticate really well. Damn."

"I'll show you any side of me you'd like, Sam Compton." She rubbed against his entire front as she breathed deep of his unique scent.

He sighed when her fingers stole beneath his shirt and caressed the hard muscles of his back. "Tempting."

"But you don't plan to take me up on it, do you?" She roamed around to his chest, then down his belly toward the fastening of his pants.

"It was just a game." He tried to retreat.

She curled her fingers in his waistband and sank to her knees. "I was playing for keeps."

Cindi popped the button open and drew down his zipper, careful not to pinch the insistent erection helping to separate the V of denim. When she covered the solid length with her palm, he cursed.

"I thought we decided this was a bad idea?" He

banged his head against the shed wall. His shoulders hit the planks, holding him up as she explored the texture of his thick shaft down to his tight balls.

"No. I didn't *choose* anything. You dictated the timing was off. I've respected your wishes." She tugged his jeans down his thighs and shoved his shirt up that washboard abdomen until she could sprinkle kisses on either side of his dick. "It's been hard. Artificial. Limiting our friendship like this. I feel like I'm lying to you about how I feel."

"I respect you too much to do this with everything else going on. Mixed together. Tangled." He gasped when she slid her mouth over the head of his cock and sucked gently. "I don't want to screw up."

"But tonight... Maybe *I* need this. You." She licked him from root to tip before whispering against the sensitive head of his cock. "There are so many things out of my control. Let me have some power. Just a little."

"Shit, yeah." He threaded his fingers in her hair, though not to direct her motion. He allowed her to work over him, thrill him and tease him as she saw fit.

She savored the taste of him. Rich earth and spice. Some part of her finally felt balanced after enjoying the golden afternoon he'd gifted her with at the lookout. She hated owing debts.

Cindi clenched his tight ass. Her nails dug in to the thick muscle as she took him deeper into her mouth. She worked him, relishing every grunt, gasp and moan he lavished on her in response.

The urge to shove him to the floor and ride took root in her core. Somehow she realized he wasn't ready. She'd come this far. If he balked, she'd die of a blend of embarrassment and desire. Maybe if she showed him how much she craved him, laid it all on the line, he'd finally see the powerful connection they shared could burn even brighter if he allowed it.

Ever since they'd rushed to the hospital, Sam had dipped into a funk. Nothing she did or said seemed to help. Except tonight…

He came alive, thrusting into her welcoming mouth.

Why couldn't he acknowledge the comfort they could give each other?

"Yes. Shit, yes." He forgot to be gentle as she drew him closer to release. "A little harder. Right there. Just like that, kitten."

Cindi inserted one hand between her legs and rubbed her pussy as she concentrated on becoming what he needed. The tang of his pre-come, which enhanced his glide over her tongue and the roof of her mouth, fueled her passion.

She sucked him hard, deep and long.

Soon she moaned in unison with him. The verbalization spurred him higher.

"Close, Cin." He groaned and tried to pry her from his body.

As if she would abandon him now. She leaned in, swallowing him to the root as she tapped her clit. When his balls drew tight against her chin and his shaft flexed, she surrendered to the bliss enveloping her.

They climaxed together. Each pump of his come down her throat matched a clamp of her aching, empty pussy. And though her body might not have been full, her heart was. At least she'd done something for him. Given him satisfaction. Helped him relax. Finally.

"Amazing." He struggled to reclaim his breath.

A wave of relief knocked her off balance. She plopped onto the ground ungracefully at best.

"Damn. Cindi, are you all right?" He tucked himself into his pants.

"Yeah. Yeah." The rush of pleasing him, herself

too, mixed with the crescendoing effect of the whiskey she'd drunk. "Head's spinning a little, that's all."

"Come on." He offered his hand.

"Where to?" She reached for him and missed. *Whoa.*

"I'm taking you inside." He knelt and gathered her into his arms. "I'll fix you up a snack. We can talk, okay?"

"Sounds good," she mumbled against his chest as he lifted her. The floating sensation lulled her as he carried her home. And suddenly she wished she never had to leave this spot, this man or this feeling behind.

Cindi closed her eyes to savor the moment.

Sam stared at the woman passed out in his bed. Adorable, sexy, naughty and dreadful at holding her liquor. He'd covered her with a soft afghan to obscure her petite yet dangerous curves from view lest he forget his self-imposed mandates.

Nothing said he couldn't sleep with her, though. As in actually sleep. He grinned as he stripped off his clothes. Maybe if he'd had a few less shots himself, he'd have put on a pair of shorts before climbing beneath the covers beside her.

Then again, why bother?

She'd seen all of him already. Had taken all of him. And while he'd sacrifice his left nut for a repeat performance if the circumstances were different, he had to admit, holding her close—skin on skin, all night long—sounded mighty fine.

Cindi burrowed against him, sighing in her sleep as she settled onto his chest.

He couldn't believe he'd known her for less than two months. Already, he considered her his closest friend. Of course his brothers were more than pals. Still, she understood him better than even Seth or Silas most times. He loved to sit with her on the porch swing at night and discuss the places they'd been and where they'd like to visit next. Or how overrated some of the things they'd tried had turned out to be. He still couldn't figure out how she managed to be so worldly but he figured she'd open up to him in time. Until then, he'd wait her out. Women with secrets were so not his thing anymore. Belinda had taught him how dangerous those waters could be.

Cindi was different. She had to be.

If he hadn't just taken a massive step in the wrong direction.

Had he betrayed her trust?

Lost her confidence?

Tomorrow would tell. Until then, he held her close and counted their synchronized heartbeats for as long as he could force himself to stay conscious.

Sam pried his eyes open when a soft, feminine thigh glided between his legs, waking more parts of him than just his brain. "Cindi."

"Mmm." She purred, still half-asleep. "Sam?"

"Yeah, kitten. It's me." He wondered who else she expected to wake up with. Not that he had any right to pry and certainly no valid reason for the flash of jealousy that clenched his jaw.

She propped herself up on his chest, blinked her eyes open and smiled down at him. "Hi."

He chuckled. "Hi."

When she bounced with his motion, she winced. "What the heck happened to my brain?"

"Ah, that marching band would be courtesy of Mr. Jack Daniels, I'd say."

"That bastard." She dropped her head onto his shoulder once more.

Sam massaged her scalp, loving the silky feel of

173

her shoulder-length curls. He paid special attention to the purple waves. They were so pretty on her. Unexpected.

"Did we...uh?" She tensed in his arms. "I can't remember."

"Damn, I didn't realize how messed up you were. We were." He couldn't imagine her sharing another easy evening with him after he confessed. "You gave me a phenomenal blow job before you passed out. I'm sorry I used you, Cindi."

"What?" She gathered the sheet to her chest as she sat up. "When are you going to realize *I* took advantage of *you*? I went to the barn with all intentions of finding you and begging you to have your way with me. I'd attempt a second wave on your ridiculous defenses this morning if I thought it would work."

"You would? You did last night? Plan to end up like that, I mean?"

"Well, I wanted to. I don't think I would have gone through with it if it hadn't been for Lucy or Jody or..."

"Jack Daniels?" He ruffled her hair.

"Yeah." She grinned.

He had to look away when her gaze roamed along the naked expanse of his body, seeming to enjoy the manscape. Shit, if he didn't focus, he'd never explain himself well enough to ensure he protected the connection they had built.

"Truth is, Cindi, I respect you too much to do this to you. I'm sorry I carted you up here last night." He grimaced. "I should have taken you home. Put you in your own bed. I just...couldn't."

"Sam Compton, are you even listening to me?" She grabbed a pillow and smashed it over his head. "What the hell am I wasting my breath for?

"Oomph." He spit a feather out and shook his

head. "Cindi?"

She'd already climbed from the bed, drawn a button-down shirt from the stack of clean laundry he hadn't yet filed in his dresser and slipped it over her head. Damn, it looked sexy on her. The sight stunned him for a moment. Long enough for her to escape.

"Hang on a minute." By the time he found his shorts and yanked them over the morning wood that surely had not been enhanced—at least he tried to convince himself—by waking up with her in his arms, she'd flown down the hall. "Cindi, wait."

"I'm done sitting on hold, Sam." She shook her head as they clattered down the stairs. "Done begging, done hoping you'll notice that what's possible between us is more than ordinary. I'm not trying to trick you by offering to blow you behind the barn or charm your pants off despite how amazingly we fit together in bed. If fucking me your first night home wasn't enough to convince you how strong our chemistry is and the day on the hood of your precious Maserati didn't do it either, there's no point in beating a dead horse."

JD, Vicky, Colby, Silas, Lucy, Seth and Jody paused with their forks halfway to their mouths in the middle of Sunday morning breakfast. Steam drifted up from the forgotten pile of pancakes they'd all wrestled over moments earlier.

"Good morning, everyone." Cindi's ultra-polite tone had nothing in common with the shrill rant she'd leveled at him a moment ago. He'd have thought she donned one of her understated dresses instead of his still-creased oxford.

"Morning, Cindi," the Comptons answered as one.

"Join us?" JD held a hand toward a vacant chair.

"Only one of you could make me accept that invitation. Clearly, he's not interested." She spun around to face the offending Compton. Bitterness and frustration dialed up to max in a heartbeat. "Goodbye, Sam. Stay the hell away from me if you only plan to tease me with what I can't have. Tiny tastes here and there aren't enough to sustain me."

Vicky didn't even holler as the screen door slammed behind the petite bookkeeper.

Things were bad.

Sam's balled his hands into fists at his sides as he forced himself to stay glued to the floor instead of running after her.

"You fucked it all up now." JD shook his head. "Might as well eat breakfast while you figure out how to fix it."

His brothers looked at him with a cross between pity and fear.

"Come on, sweetie." Lucy held out her arms. She patted him on the back, then pressed him toward the empty chair next to her. "Vicky made blueberry, your favorite."

He mutilated one of the fluffy masterpieces while his family talked around him. None of the treat made it to his stomach, which threatened to revolt at any second.

What had he done?

Chapter Thirteen

Six and a half weeks after returning to Compass Ranch

Sam gawked at the icon flashing in his system tray. He hadn't bothered to uninstall the firm's video conferencing software from his laptop. Who the hell would be trying to reach him?

He hovered his cursor over the cancel button. Curiosity got the better of him. He finger-combed his hair—damn, it'd gotten long—spit-shined the camera embedded in frame around his laptop screen and connected the link to find his old boss on the other end. "Gandle."

"Sam! Wow, you're looking...different." The stuffy bastard adjusted his conservative maroon tie. "Glad you're awake. Wasn't sure what time it was out there in Montana."

"Wyoming."

"Right." He laughed.

Sam wondered how he'd ever envied the partners' slick yet surface-deep interest in their clients and employees.

"Well, you always were a hard worker. In fact, now that you've had some time to cool off, we were wondering if you'd like to put some of that elbow grease into the fund you spoke of."

"The one you didn't believe was mine? What changed?" Sam kicked back in his chair, propping his ankles on the support bar beneath his desk. "Why the sudden turnaround? One minute you're practically accusing me of rape and the next...my job is up for grabs again. I may have been that naïve two months ago. No more."

"Damn, son."

Sam gritted his teeth. This man had nothing in common with his father.

"You're better at this game than I thought. When I'm wrong, I say so. Belinda..." He cleared his throat. "Attempted to play her little tricks on me, same as she did to you."

"I hope you at least got a decent blow job out of her before she reamed your ass." Sam couldn't stop himself from being crass. Good thing Vicky had run into town for groceries.

The partner huffed out a derisive laugh. "I've had hotter treats from the popsicle cart on Forty-Second Street."

"Glad to know it wasn't me." Sam shook his head. "I'm not about to waste any more of our time. I'm not interested in making money for you."

"You're not?" Gandle's jaw dropped open. Had anyone ever told him no before?

"Nope." Sam relished the moment.

"Opening the fund was important to you. I could see it on your face that morning."

"Oh, it still is. Actually, the day I snatched the foundational securities at bargain basement prices was a pretty awesome personal milestone." He beamed.

"Performance indicators are top notch so far. Sure, I couldn't buy as big as I had planned, but the payoff is enormous when I'm not sharing the profits."

"You already made your trades?" Gandle closed his eyes for a moment. "I don't suppose you want to share your picks? We'll give them buy recommendations, boost the prices for you."

"Nah. I'm good, thanks." Sam reached toward the button that would sever the connection.

"Wait."

Sam's finger dangled over the Escape key.

"What would it take?" Gandle swiped at beads of sweat dotting his forehead.

"For what?" Sam leaned in closer.

"To get you back on our side. VP? No, hell, we'll promote you to president."

"I don't think…"

"Fine. Partner." Gandle grimaced. "Smith can be encouraged to retire if necessary."

"You'd do that to someone you've worked with for fifteen years?" Sam shook his head. How could this have been his dream? Belinda had done him a huge favor. "Thanks, but no thanks, *sir*."

"Son of a bitch." A one of a kind pen launched across the room. "Without you or Belinda we have no shot in cornering this market."

"Hang on. What'd you say?" Could he have heard that right? "Where'd Belinda go? Did you fire her for her sexual shenanigans?"

"Hardly." A terse snort echoed in the executive's mammoth office. "I'd have banged her, no hardship there. She got cocky. Played her hand too soon. Thought she had investors lined up and bolted to bigger, shinier seas. They didn't have the cash they'd promised her to play with."

Well that explained why all his preferred stocks

had remained available and reasonably priced while he sorted out his family issues. Too bad, so sad.

Sam grinned.

"You might want to dial that shit down, son. Last I heard, the barracuda was on a flight heading your way. Actually, I called because I thought she'd already be there. Maybe she wants to kiss and make up."

"Thanks for the early warning." Sam grimaced.

"It's the least I could do." Gandle shrugged. "Don't take it personal, Sam. It was about business. Always about protecting our assets."

"Funny. I'd sacrifice every liquefiable interest I have to keep my family intact. I'd gladly fork over every dime if I could buy my dad more time. All of us. I can't believe I forgot what was really important. Thanks for reminding me."

"Sam—"

He punched the end button, silencing the objection of his one-time mentor.

A huge weight lifted off his shoulders. He didn't doubt for one moment he'd done the right thing by coming home. He only regretted that he hadn't acted sooner. He could have spent more time with JD. Vicky. His brothers. Cindi.

Shit.

How many years had he wasted? Maybe he should make up for it now instead of deferring his relationship with Cindi until some mystical ideal period in his life. Reality was, there would never be a perfect time. Things could go haywire without notice. It'd be better to have her by his side than to muddle through on his own. Hell, he'd forced her to suffer alone these past few weeks.

No more. He shoved his chair back from the desk and marched toward the barn. He'd think of something to say by the time he got to Cindi's office. Except, when he burst onto the porch, a rental sedan sat dead center in the yard, hogging the free space.

"Oh no." He broke into a run, loping toward the disaster he could sense brewing like an experiment gone wrong in a mad scientist's laboratory.

He cleared the entryway and paused to let his pupils dilate. Feminine insults rang from the far end of the aisle way.

"You're that bitch, Belinda?" Cindi sounded ready to spit. "Hell fucking no I won't tell you where to find Sam. Hit the road and take that last-season bag with you."

"Do you have any idea how much this cost?" Belinda reeled as though someone had punched her in the stomach instead of insulting her purse.

"Doesn't make it any less fugly." Cindi put her nose in the air and sniffed.

The awkward angle left her vulnerable to Belinda when she swung the truly hideous gold-leather at Cindi's face.

Before Sam could yell out a warning, the heavy satchel caught her on the jaw. She sputtered, then pounced, knocking Belinda off her ridiculously high heels into the pile of hay nearby. A cloud of dust enveloped the women as they struggled for the top position.

Sam gaped so wide you could have driven a tractor through his mouth.

Screeches ricocheted through the space while they wrestled, putting the hen house at feeding time to shame.

"Holy girl fight!" Colby shoved past the cowboys gathering on the other side of the barn. The sight of his friend racing toward the women spurred Sam to motion.

He reached the tangle of smooth skin and silky hair first, unsure of how to begin.

"Grab Cindi." Colby waved his hands toward the flash of purple. "I'll take the tall one."

Sam wrapped his arms around Cindi's waist and hauled her upright. Colby did the same to Belinda. Her elbow caught him in the nose, and he jerked. "Son of a bitch."

Blood trickled over Colby's lip.

"Enough, kitten," Sam crooned, trying to calm Cindi. Her ferocious defense had his cock hard in the small of her back. She would stick up for him even after he'd hurt her? "Maybe I should call you wildcat from now on."

"Sam." Belinda went from tigress to simpering victim in half a second. Mascara streaked as she manufactured tears. "You're going to let that cunt hit me?"

"Pretty sure you deserved it, honey." Sam relished Cindi's undignified snort. He ran his hands over her body, making sure nothing seemed out of place. If Belinda had so much as scratched her, he'd press charges. Somehow he doubted prison garb lived up to her fashion standards.

"You know her?" Colby held Belinda with straight arms, as if she stunk worse than the pigpen on a hot day.

"Thought I did." Sam shook his head. "Belinda was just leaving."

"But, Samuel..." she pleaded. "Hear me out. I have a proposition for you."

"Gross. I just bet you do." Cindi wrinkled her adorable nose, scrunching together the freckles dusting the bridge.

Sam chuckled and picked hay from the lavender locks below his chin.

"There's nothing you have that I want, Belinda." Sam shook his head. "Gandle beat you to it. He filled me in. Looks like you shot yourself in those Manolo Blahniks."

"But—" She might have kept arguing if an enormous sneeze hadn't shaken her skeletal frame.

How had he ever found her attractive?

"Allergies." She sniffled, horrified when her nose began to run. "Hay. Cats. Horses. Dust. Gah!"

Another sneeze rocked her on her inappropriate heels.

Cindi squirmed from his hold to retrieve a box from her office. Despite their rude introduction, she offered the other woman a tissue. Belinda knocked the cardboard from Cindi's hands.

"Have it your way." Cindi rounded on him. "Really? *Her*? You slept with her, but me you're not interested in?"

"Cindi, wait..." Sam reached for her hand, intent on convincing her he'd come out here to beg for another chance.

"Cindi?" Belinda cocked her head in between another round of sneezes. "Wait a minute... I thought you looked familiar. How many women would opt for those nasty highlights? Just didn't think you'd be hiding all the way out here. Are you telling me you're Cindi—"

The bookkeeper froze. Her wild stare winged from Belinda to Sam to Colby. Before she could utter another sound, Belinda was ushered from the barn by Colby, who yelled over the snake's continued rant, "I've got this under control, Sam. I'll see your guest back to the airport."

"Thanks." He never took his eyes from Cindi.

She smiled faintly, wringing her hands and staring after Colby and the blotchy, red-faced version of Belinda.

"Planning to tell me what that was all about?"

183

Sam cocked his head. Where would Belinda have possibly met Cindi before? The world wasn't *that* small after all.

"No." She studied the ground as she shuffled toward her office.

"Cindi." Sam grabbed her wrist. "I came out here to admit I messed up. I'm ready. I'd like to try for something big with you. But if you don't trust me, how can that work?"

"Trust? I'm not the one with issues there." She avoided his stare. "What would I have to hide?"

"I don't know, kitten." He cupped her cheek in his hand, rubbing his thumb over a smudge of dirt left behind from her scuffle. "From me, I don't think there's reason to keep secrets. I'll give you the same understanding you've shown me. I swear."

She shook her head. "What if it's too much for you to handle? What if you run again?"

"I don't scare easily," he murmured. "I'm here for you."

"I can't."

Sam felt as though someone had dunked him in the lake in the middle of February. He'd almost made the same mistake twice. Ready to open up and lay himself bare before a woman who couldn't do the same for him.

"If you change your mind, you know where to find me." He kissed her cheek. "Think about it, okay?"

He didn't give her a chance to respond before he spun and left the barn. So much for his grand designs.

Chapter Fourteen

Eight weeks after returning to Compass Ranch

JD had announced his official retirement at dinner. Today had been his last day in the pastures.

Ever.

He'd arranged to transfer responsibility to Colby, Silas, Seth and Sam in front of the hands first thing in the morning. Vicky, Lucy, Jody and Cindi planned to attend the informal gathering. They'd invited all the other staff and neighbors to share in a surprise potluck buffet afterward. A few of their friends had asked to make brief speeches.

Sam slammed the side of his hand into the dresser. Dealing with the daily decline of JD had turned out to be harder than he imagined. Especially while surrounded by the partnership of his parents, Silas, Colby and Lucy as well as Seth and Jody. He figured he should have had *odd man out* tattooed beside his fancy E. Christ, there was so much love in the air it made him sick with envy. What kind of fuckwad resented the happiness of his family?

Especially in times like these.

Things had been easier before Cindi cut him off. At least then he'd had a willing ear whenever he'd needed it. What kind of pussy did it make him that he'd been ready to cherish her friendship and instead she turned him down when he didn't marry the offer of a shoulder to cry on with stud service?

Christ. Yet somehow every member of his family seemed to think their meltdown had been his fault. He'd suffered lectures from JD, Vicky, his brothers, their mates—all of them piled on the poor-Cindi bandwagon.

He had to get out of here. If only for a little while. He'd take Dee and roam the night like he'd done after he'd forgotten to latch the gate on the coyote-proof pen and they'd lost three lambs to the hunters when he'd been fourteen. Only then, he'd had Sawyer to keep him company. His twin had sensed his self-directed anger and sadness. He'd ridden, quiet for once, by Sam's side.

Too bad for them all, he'd had it.

Sam was calling his brother. This time he wasn't giving up until they spoke. The guy had a right to know, to share these last days with their father. Every one that passed marked a deterioration for JD—a little slower, a little sleepier, a little more pain-ridden. And there was nothing they could do but keep him company as he descended.

Sam reached in his pocket and drew out his cell phone. It took three tries before he could swipe the touchscreen in the necessary pattern to unlock the display. He punched the contact folder, then Sawyer's ridiculous profile picture from Facebook, which he'd saved to display every time Saw called.

A deep breath rattled his ribs. Then another.

The phone lowered as he stared at the screen, which blurred in his watery stare. No messages, no texts, no nothing. So much for the prickle in his neck, which he'd swear had been telling him all day Sawyer might already be back on dry land. Although he probably would have called to check in, he might also be out partying and fucking himself into oblivion after so long at sea.

"Screw it." Sam mashed the icon and hauled the device to his ear.

It rang.

And rang.

And rang some more.

Until Sawyer's cheery begging to leave a message and a phone number to call back had Sam half-laughing along with his half-definitely-not-crying.

The transmission severed with a beep an instant before he redialed. *Answer me.*

Halfway through the second ring, Sawyer picked up. The slight pant in his greeting confirmed Sam's suspicions. "Dude. Really? Twice? I'm sort of busy…"

"Uh, sorry." *Holy shit!* Sam was so surprised to hear Sawyer he couldn't drum up a thing to say.

"Sam? What is it? Is Silas okay? Shit, I should have called. It's just…" The instant fluctuation from relaxed to tense changed Sam's mind. He couldn't sign up for torturing his brother. The rest of them had agonized enough.

Also known as chickening out.

"Si? Oh yeah, how would I know? Haven't heard anything from him in weeks. He's fine I'm sure." Sam laughed. "Sorry, must have butt dialed."

"Twice? Talented ass you've got, bro."

The dulcet tones of a female voice filtered through the speaker.

"Yeah, I hear how busy you are. Let you get back to it…her, I mean. Have fun. Be safe."

"I'll call you in the morning." Sawyer paused. "You're sure everything's good?"

"Yep. Other than you stalling for your girl. Hope

you're not losing your wood."

"Don't you worry about my cock, okay? Damn. Gotta go."

The picture of Sawyer on Sam's phone was replaced with a giant red X.

Sam banged his head on the wall several times in a row. He jammed the device in his pocket and tore along the hallway. Night air would do him some good. The back door squeaked loud as ever, though he shut it softly before racing down the stairs and jogging toward the barn. Fired up, he didn't notice the lights streaming from beneath the not-quite-shut door until he was less than ten feet away.

"What the fuck—?"

A loud cry rent the night. A feminine shout was followed by male grunts and groans. Holy shit, was someone being attacked in there? He ripped the panel open with enough force to shake the entire wall of the barn. A swarm of cowboys surrounded a petite woman with platinum and lavender streaked hair.

Cindi.

Sam could use a good fight right about now. He cracked his knuckles before clenching his fists. If they'd harmed even one of those wild hairs on her head, he'd rip them limb from limb despite the fact there had to be more than a half dozen of the strapping guys.

"Get the fuck off her. Right now!"

He didn't expect her soft response, more question than grateful relief. "Sam? Is that you?"

Could she be enjoying this?

He shook his head, clearing the irrational rage and measuring the scene objectively. Guys framed her with their cocks in hand. They didn't pin her down. Instead, they supported her, held her up and open for their buddies, who filled her seeking hands, mouth and pussy.

Fantasies collided before him as though someone had made a 3D porno out of his greatest desires and cast his favorite actress in the starring role. Sam had no choice—he had to investigate.

Cindi froze with one hand on Jake's cock and tried to close her legs around Duke, as he plowed between her creamy thighs. He'd built long and slow to this final sprint and she hated stealing his glory. Considerate and gentle, he always tended to her pleasure before seeking his own. He shouldn't have to suffer this rude interruption.

Sam refused to be ignored.

Would he damn her, rail and shout or could he possibly understand? Even a little.

She shivered as she prayed.

"This?" He smacked his palm on his thigh hard enough it had to burn all through his elbow. "*This* is the secret you've been hiding from me? You like to get nasty? Fuck the hands? Let them pass you around. Give yourself to them all…"

"Sam." Jake angled his torso to protect Cindi from the brunt of Sam's ire. "Careful how you talk to her. Don't disrespect her or you'll find yourself facedown in the hay. I don't have a problem kicking the boss's son's ass any more now than I did when you were a spoiled kid."

"You could try." Sam swallowed hard.

Still, Jake let Sam pass. *Interesting.*

She allowed the men—Johnny below her, Duke between her legs, Levi, Jake and a couple others she couldn't place scattered around—to support her as she absorbed Sam's inspection.

The searing beam of his gaze scanned her from head to toe.

"You let them come on you?" He studied the

slick trail of pearly come decorating one of her breasts. The lines had never shamed her before. They didn't this time either when Sam's pupils dilated as though the sight alone made him yearn to mark her, too. "Does it turn you on? How many times can they make you shatter before they're wasted?"

He elbowed Levi out of his path.

His focus returned some of the steam to Cindi's core. Her pussy clenched on Duke, and her thighs trembled in his big hands.

"I need them." She closed her eyes and Johnny, who'd volunteered to act as a human couch to prevent her from lying on the floor of the barn, surrounded her in a bear hug.

"I've got you, doll." He murmured in her ear, "We need you too."

"So, what, you thought I'd flip? That I wouldn't think it's hot?" He stalked closer to trail a finger through the iridescent proof icing her breast.

She bit her lip and nodded, furious at the tears that sprang to her eyes, unshed. "I was willing to give them up for you. But you didn't want me."

The cowboys grumbled at both halves of her revelation.

"Not true. I didn't think I could have you. If I had known this…"

"Would it have been different?" She shook her head. "No. Your focus still would have been on JD. I get that."

"How could I ignore *this*? It was hard enough when I thought you were perfect in every way but one. You have no idea what seeing you like this does to me. I need too, Cindi. So bad. I never would have guessed you had this in common with me. Though I suppose I should have, like everything else. Shit. All we did was waste our time." Sam ripped his flannel shirt from his powerful frame. Dear God he had a body on him. So much different than the men surrounding her. Not any less muscular yet so much more refined. Skewed from bulk to sinew. "I'm going to fuck you so every man here can witness how you come apart for me."

Duke began to retreat from her pussy.

She whimpered. Greedy. She craved them all. Dreams of Sam joining their midnight rendezvous had haunted her from the first day she'd spotted him climbing from the ranch's pick-up like a model from the cowboy edition of *GQ*. The blend of his cosmopolitan appeal and his rugged decency had tripped her up from the instant they'd made eye contact across the yard.

"Don't stop on my account, boys." Sam opened his arms. "Show me what she likes. Then watch me blow her away."

"You always were a pretentious little shit." Jake smacked Sam on the ass. "You don't know what you're digging yourself into this time, preppy."

"We'll see about that." Sam tugged open his button fly and extracted the hard-on she'd spotted growing along his thigh. He stroked himself with strong, sure passes of his non-calloused fingers.

It'd been a long time since smooth hands had caressed her.

Jake looked to her for approval.

She always had the final say on who joined their groupings. Before she parted her lips and invited Jake back inside her mouth, she nodded.

Sam grinned, then stepped closer. "You wouldn't believe the things I learned while I was away, Jake."

She couldn't be safer, surrounded by men who respected and cherished her despite her penchant for ménage. Unlike her family, the cowboys wouldn't abandon her even if Sam suddenly decided he didn't approve of her wanton behavior once he'd satisfied his own lust.

Cindi shivered.

"Ease up. You're scaring her, asshole." Jake smacked Sam in the gut even as he sank farther into her open mouth.

She suckled on the head of his cock, drawing the familiar flavor of him across her taste buds to erase the memories threatening to assault her. Her mind blanked, and she surrendered to instinct, curling her toes and digging her heels into Duke's ass.

"That's right, sweetheart." Jake crooned to her as he fed her more of his shaft. "It's always better for you if you clear those thoughts from your mind. You think too damn much."

Instead of arguing, she absorbed his feedback. Muscles relaxed, her jaw opened wider.

Sam smiled, putting his hands on her chest. He didn't fondle her breasts or zip straight to her nipples like he was using them to jumpstart a dead battery. No, he massaged her, rubbing the tension from the muscles below and up to her shoulders. She hummed around Jake.

"Damn." The cowboy gnashed his teeth.

"I thought you'd hang on longer than that, Jake. Should have known you were a three-second wonder." Sam laughed when Jake shot him a nasty glare. "Then again, I know how tempting this pretty mouth is."

Cindi twitched when Sam traced her stretched lips around the girth of Jake's respectable cock. Holy shit. He had no reservations.

"Oh, hell yeah." Duke's moan drew their attention. He resumed his somewhat unsteady pumping. His dark olive shaft disappeared as her lighter flesh swallowed him whole. "She's into that. Strangling me."

"Do the guys ever touch each other for you,

kitten?"

Her eyes grew wide. She cruised up and down Jake's throbbing shaft when she shook her head no.

"Nice. All their effort is for you." He nodded. "Maybe someday we'll ask Colby and Si to give you a treat. I bet Lucy would love to show them off."

"Don't give her any ideas. She doesn't need help being naughty. Cindi prefers being watched." Levi changed positions, securing an open spot on the other side of her torso. He rubbed her belly with gentle strokes that seemed out of context for the big man. He never ceased to amaze her with his tenderness. "Hurry, guys, Duke is on the edge."

Sam tuned into the urgency. He dropped to his knees beside her and mirrored Levi's caresses. The men had studied how best to please her and didn't mind educating their friend.

"She likes to come with each of us." Levi smiled up at her. "We love it too. Knowing she's as into it as we are. She's so generous. Here, pet her like this."

Levi grabbed Sam's hand and aligned it over her mound.

Cindi's eyes rolled when they plied her together.

"Yeah." Duke grunted with each hitch of his hips. "Close, Cin. It's too much. Always too much with you. So sweet."

Two of the other ranchers supported her legs, taking the burden off of Duke's elbows. He used his freedom to enhance the delight pulsing outward from the spot where Sam rubbed her clit. Duke painted big swirls on the undersides of her thighs with his fingers as he flexed his hips, shoving long and deep within her.

"Bet that feels good, kitten." Sam alternated between monitoring Duke's progress and checking her reaction. "He's fucking you nice and deep, isn't he?"

She smiled around Jake's cock.

"I've got this." Sam shooed Levi from her pussy, leaving the cowboy to focus on her breasts.

He always had been a tit man.

Levi plumped her sensitive chest. He rubbed the lingering come into her skin, making it shine before he closed his teeth lightly around her distended nipple.

Though she'd already come four or five times, a rush of forbidden desire rekindled the embers of her desire. Stealing a glance into Sam's gorgeous green eyes would have been enough to set her ablaze. The tip of his tongue snaking out to flirt with his finger over her clit did her in. Especially when Duke's thrusts made Sam's licking inconsistent.

Jake withdrew from her mouth, careful of her teeth when she screamed.

Duke rammed inside once more and locked deep. His face turned purple as he pumped the condom he wore full of his come.

She wrung spurt after spurt from his ultra-hard cock, loving how the defined ridge of his head prodded her in all the right places as she hugged him tight. Long after he'd begun to soften, she continued to quake.

"You want in next, Sam?" Jake's offer came out a little ragged. She encouraged his downward spiral by reaching out her tongue to lap his balls.

"Thanks, but no."

Cindi's heart stuttered. What the hell did he mean, *no*?

"Sam…" Jake's fingers tightened in her hair when she began to retreat.

"I mean, you're not going to last long enough. If you want to ride her you'd better go ahead. Besides, I believe in saving the best for last." He kissed her tummy in a gentle promise. Couldn't he tell he'd already made it better than ever?

Jake barked a laugh. "We'll see about that."

Cindi worried she might have to keep Jake in line when she left with Sam tonight. But when she glanced up at him, he winked. Typical guys, giving each other shit. Could everyone see how much Sam affected her? Everyone but him?

"Levi?" Sam tagged the man feasting at her chest. "Why don't you go at the same time?"

His raised eyebrows had Cindi swallowing a chuckle.

"You telling me you'd be disappointed with sliding your dick through her cleavage?" Sam shook his head when Levi bared his teeth in a lusty hiss. "I didn't think so. Show her how much you like that sexy rack."

"Hell, yeah." He leaned in for a quick kiss before straddling her torso.

Johnny beat her to plumping her breasts. He reached around from beneath her to squish the mounds together enough to form a valley perfect for sandwiching Levi's hard-on.

From the corner of her eye, she spotted Jake snagging a condom from the pile in someone's upturned hat. He sheathed himself with practiced ease. The head of Levi's cock nudged her cleavage, nestling between her breasts as Jake insinuated himself between her thighs. Larger than Duke, who'd collapsed against one of the stalls to watch the action, he spread her wider.

"He's going to stretch you, Cin." Sam licked his lips as he watched the men pleasure her. He seemed twice as turned on by absorbing her ecstasy than he had any of the times he'd sought his own gratification with her. "Are you ready for him?"

Sam stroked her hip, then walked his fingers to her pussy. He parted her lips, helping Jake to notch his cock in the perfect position for penetration.

With Levi hovering over her torso, she couldn't

see Jake. It didn't matter. The only man she cared about was the one orchestrating her pleasure. She turned her head and stared into Sam's eyes.

"God, yes. Put him inside me." She flung out her arm and squeezed Sam's shoulder. "I want to show you what we're capable of."

"Don't worry, kitten. You're already the hottest thing I've ever seen." He groaned when Jake advanced through his fingers, and she gasped. "I can't wait to fuck you while they watch. I've never been so hard in all my life."

She peeked at his crotch, then licked her lips. For the first time ever, she wished Jake and Levi would hurry. She needed Sam. Wanted him to claim her in front of the rest of the cowboys. Maybe then she'd believe this was real and not another dream.

"Want me to suck you?" She remembered often how hard he'd come in her mouth.

"Not tonight. I want to watch." He rubbed her tummy below Levi's thighs. "Enjoy yourself, Cindi. Let me see how good they make you feel."

"Enough talking." Jake growled, then buried himself another inch or two in her pussy. Though she'd just come, she hit a zone where pleasure ebbed and flowed rather than slamming her with discrete orgasms. Only sharing like this could bring her to this place. It didn't happen every time, but when it did it was sublime.

Levi licked his palm, then rubbed the valley of her breasts, easing his forward passage. Two of the other cowboys inched closer, stroking their cocks near her shoulders as they shared in the energy they generated together. Their guttural chants and the speed of their fingers, flashing over their erections, could have only one outcome.

"Want some help with that, Levi?" Cindi put one

hand on each of the men and angled their hips so their cocks aimed at her chest.

"Shit." He looked up from where the head of his cock now peeked from between the top curve of her breasts long enough to clue in to her proposal. "Yeah. Get her slick for me."

No sooner had he vocalized the idea, then the first warm rivulet painted over her breast and tricked onto Levi's cock. He thrust, spreading the natural lubrication along his glide path.

"That's right, kitten." Sam's hand trembled where he infused her with his heat. "Look how much they want you."

The second cowboy joined his friend. Together they coated her chest, Johnny's assisting hands and Levi's shaft with jet after jet of come. Soon the cowboy slid effortlessly between the plump softness molded around him. Spent, the two donors kissed her cheeks before joining the spectators against the other wall.

"Ah, damn." Levi shook his head from side to side. "Gorgeous. Perfect."

Jake distracted her with the forward motion of his hips. His cock embedded in her to the root. His pelvis trapped her clit. He rocked in a series of short strokes deep within her, tapping a bundle of nerves. Her back arched, giving Levi more room to play.

When she turned her head, Sam's stare set her soul on fire. He smiled at her, approval radiating from every pore of his slightly sweaty skin. He looked as though he burned, like she did.

"Kiss me?" She reached for him but he had already lurched toward her face.

His palms cupped her cheeks and he stared into her eyes as one man fucked her chest and another wreaked havoc on her from the inside out. With Johnny's arms around her, his hard body protecting her back, Jake possessing her pussy and Levi stroking her chest, she'd never felt so safe, so secure or so sure of her place.

"I finally feel like I'm really home," Sam whispered against her lips, for her ears only. "With you, I have everything I need. Together we can make this our place. Forever."

"Yes." She wished she could tell him more of what was in her heart, but it'd swollen so huge it choked her. Instead, she stretched her neck upward, laying her mouth over his.

Tenderness hit her, amplifying the effect of the physical sensations bombarding her. She clenched on Jake's cock, quaking with the force of another climax.

"Cin," he shouted as he slammed into her, rocking all of them with the force of his thrusts. "Coming."

"Fuck." Levi slapped the head of his dick on first one of her nipples, then the other before reinserting it between her breasts. "Me too. Can't stop."

They rode her furiously, pouring themselves into her, onto her.

Throughout the storm of emotions, passion and pleasure, Sam kissed her. He remained gentle, coaxing her orgasm to linger. It was long minutes before she realized her skin began to cool. Levi had left, and Jake knelt beside her. "Thank you, Cindi."

"You're always welcome, Jake."

"Not like this. It's different with Sam here. Better. More important." He struggled to catch his breath.

Levi returned with his discarded shirt. He cleaned her chest as best he could with his suddenly uncoordinated limbs. "Will you let us watch him make love to you? I think it's something we've all fantasized about."

She glanced to Sam one last time. He nodded.

"Me too." She laughed, unable to believe this was really happening. Not only did Sam want her. Not only did he find her kinks sexy. Not only did he take her to new heights. But he planned to claim her. Publicly.

"Lift her up." Sam directed his order at Jake, then swung around to face the crowd. "All of you. Help. Hold her for me. Brace her while I make her mine."

Cindi yelped when Johnny shifted below her. He raised her into Jake's eager grasp. She put out her arms as he settled her with her shoulders against his chest. Levi and Duke ducked beneath her arms, which clung to their broad shoulders. Hands boosted her—on her ass, her thighs, her knees, her ankles and even her feet—until she floated, borne by the men surrounding her.

Sam rose, unfolding his powerful frame. He kicked off his boots, then stripped his jeans away before stalking toward her. As he approached, the sea of hands moved as one, parting her legs and lowering her torso until she reclined comfortably in their grasp.

They presented her to Sam.

Could they feel the bond arcing between her and Sam, stronger with every beat of their hearts? Did they sense the unyielding rightness she did whenever he came near? Would they listen to any man if he weren't the true master of her soul?

She didn't think so.

Sam stroked his cock from root to tip as he situated himself at the juncture of her thighs. Still he never looked away from her eyes.

"Will you take me, Cindi?" He paused, and she knew she could crush him in that instant. She held all the power. Except that hurting him would only hurt her more. She couldn't deny it anymore. In eight short weeks, she'd fallen in love with this man.

"I already have." She smiled through the tears in her eyes. "Now take me. Please."

Sam mingled curse with prayer as he pressed inside her.

The hands cupping her shifted, dropping her low and tight to her lover, easing his advance through her swollen channel. They murmured approval as she tightened. Before he'd inserted the full length of his long, thick cock, she disintegrated. Orgasm crashed through her, over and over as he rode the waves from the very entrance of her clamping pussy to the depths of her channel. He fucked her so deep she wondered how he didn't end up smothered by her welcoming grasp.

A sea of chanted encouragement egged them both on. Sam rode her, driving her from peak to peak until she lost count of how many times she tumbled into rapture. He picked up the pace, flying over her, his face contorted in a mask of need and agony.

"Let go, Sam," she called to him. "Join me. Stay with me. Love me."

"I. Do." He threw back his head, the cords of his neck impressing her with their prominent strength. "Do. Cindi."

He erupted deep within her. The animalistic grace with which he pumped her full inspired one last round of spasms in her pussy. Cindi cried out with him, the pleasure enhanced when she realized the scalding spray inside of her was his come. He hadn't worn a condom. Hadn't put even that tiny barrier between them.

Nothing could separate them after tonight.

Bonded.

Permanent.

"Yeah," he whispered as he stared into her eyes. "Exactly what you're thinking. Same goes."

Chapter Fifteen

Sam hugged Cindi to his chest as they crested the rise and shifted to the downhill portion of their journey, trickier when riding bareback and double. Dee went slow, careful not to throw her charges. Cindi melted into his embrace, conforming to every plane and hollow of his body as though she'd been tailor-made for him.

Hell, how could he believe she hadn't been?

Sam slid from Dee's back, then lowered Cindi to the carpet of wildflowers in front of the cottage. He secured the animal, making sure she had plenty of room to graze and a fresh bucket of water before trailing Cindi up the stairs.

He didn't know what to expect when her hand paused on the knob and she glanced over her shoulder with her bottom lip between her teeth.

"Go ahead. What, are you a slob or something?" His whole family teased him about his neat freak tendencies.

"Hell, no." She laughed. "You're right. I'm being silly. After tonight…"

"Yeah." He would have kissed her, but then they'd end up making love under the moon and stars instead of in her soft bed. He figured he owed her a proper mattress at least one of these times.

She nodded, then let the door swing open.

Sam whistled as he stepped inside. He hadn't expected this.

It wasn't a simple shack. Nor was it opulent or gaudy in the least. More like the refined tastes of someone who knows what's worth spending cash on and what's hyped up garbage. Items had been selected with discerning style and investments made in ultra-elite components that counted most like the marble flooring, which must have radiant heat embedded in it to stay warm to the touch of his socked feet.

"Damn nice place." He shook his head. "I see why you don't let anyone check it out."

"Why are you thinking?" Her tight question made him select his response carefully.

"They'd realize how much stuff you've let other guys buy you." He shrugged as though it didn't make bile climb his esophagus. Cindi wasn't all that different from Belinda after all. Sure, she flared where his ex had frozen. In the end, both women used their bodies to separate men from their better sense, their jobs and their wallets. "Is that the agreement you alluded to with JD? He pays you a pittance since he knows you're picking up business on the side?"

"Did you just imply that I'm a whore?" The set of her shoulders clued him in to what he'd see when she rounded on him. Furious eyes, a firm mouth and denial ready to spill from her swollen, well-fucked lips.

He ignored the feigned injury in her glare. Could she have expected him to be okay with how she used her fuck buddies? Stupid. Such a moronic romantic, he assumed she'd given herself with such abandon because it filled a void in her soul, not her pocketbook.

"Well, that's a strong word. I suppose you're

more of a trader. It's not every day a man finds someone willing to slake his unusual desires out here in the middle of nowhere."

Her breasts rose and fell as she took one deep breath, then another.

Shit, he couldn't insult her when he'd partaken of the spoils. But his heart cracked and he swore he wouldn't show it. Not again.

"I don't blame you for making a life for yourself." Sam scratched his chin. "Makes more sense now, really. I never saw you as a good fit for that dusty office in the barn. Now I know why you hang out there. Advertising. Flaunting yourself has to be good for—"

He barely ducked the vase she hurled in his direction. It landed on the sleek couch with austere lines that spoke of high-quality design. Good thing too. The vessel looked like the swirled Venetian glass of an original Dale Chihuly. Pricey.

"Sam Compton, get the hell out of my house." She charged toward him, brandishing a solid silver candelabra.

"Whoa." He backpedaled, hands raised, palms facing out. "No need for violence."

"There is. If you don't leave in the next ten seconds I swear I'll...I'll call your dad."

Hardball. "Jesus. Don't wake JD. I'm leaving. Too bad. I was looking forward to spending the night showing you how good it can be in private."

"With a woman you think is no better than a flesh peddler?" She sneered. "What does that make you, Sam?"

"A moron, obviously." He couldn't argue with her. After suffering the burn of embarrassment once, why would he leave himself open to being shafted again?

With his fingers on the doorknob, he paused at

the sound of her raspy whisper. "No, that's me. I thought I might have finally found someone who wouldn't judge. Someone I could have adventures with and keep to myself when I felt the need for some alone time. When the hell will I learn it's not possible? That man does not exist."

"Cindi—"

"Ten…. Nine…"

"Fuck." He couldn't restrain the anger, pain, misery and loss—so much loss—from lashing out at her. "I'll stop by the barn tomorrow with that bottle of *L'heure Bleue*. Probably owe you a lifetime supply, but it'll have to do for now."

He slammed the door to her chic cottage to shut out the mutilation he'd inflicted and keep himself from running back inside to kiss away the tears streaming down her cheeks.

Sam angled his head to glare at the coffee pot when the auto-brew feature kicked in. Wake up calls came dark and fucking early at four-thirty in the morning on the ranch. He'd sat at the dining room table for hours, unable to consider sleep with so much bitterness churning in his guts.

He picked at the edge of the placemat before him when JD stumbled into the kitchen. He rushed to his father's side and helped him situate himself at the table. "When are you going to start using that walker Lucy brought you?"

"I'd rather crack my head open walking under my own steam, thanks."

"Impossible to dent that thick skull of yours, I bet." Sam shook his head, grabbed the first cup of coffee and fixed it with a spoonful of sugar for JD, then plopped down once more.

"One of the many ways you and I are alike, son."

JD put his hand on Sam's wrist, stilling his incessant tapping. His dad's fingers were gnarled and the joints looked huge in proportion to the rest of him, which seemed to shrink day by day. "Gonna tell me what's had you huffing and puffing out here like an old lady all night?"

"Heard that, did you?"

"Hard not to. So, let me guess. Woman trouble?" JD frowned.

"Cindi," Sam confirmed.

"Ah, yeah." JD smiled. "I heard you storm out to the barn earlier. I suppose you finally figured out how much you really have in common?"

"What would you know about—" Sam stopped himself short. JD knew everything.

"What I can't understand is why you're here, instead of snug in the cottage." JD grimaced. "I expected the two of you to be as over the top as Seth and Jody or Si and his pair. What's the damn hold up now?"

"I can't believe you'd want me to end up with her, knowing…"

JD's white eyebrows climbed. "That she's passionate? Loyal? Fierce yet delicate?"

"A hooker."

"What!" JD clenched his middle and bellowed with laughter. Until he realized Sam didn't join him. "You're fucking kidding me, right?"

"You must know." Sam scrubbed his hand over his eyes. "When's the last time you were inside Aunt Meade's cottage?"

"*Cindi's* cottage." JD leaned forward. "Two days ago I stopped by to check on her. She hasn't been the same since that bitch followed you from the East Coast. Something has her skittish."

"So you've seen what she's done to the place."

Sam tilted his head. Frustration bubbled to the surface. "How do you explain that luxury on the pathetic salary you pay her?"

"Oh."

"Yeah. Fucking *oh* is right." Sam uncurled his fingers from the fork in front of him when the tines began to bend.

"Enough is enough already." JD thumped his fist on the table. "You two are screwing everything up. Look, Sam, your girl has been all over the world, she knows about your fancy shit and can afford anything she damn well pleases. If she had her way, she'd work for free. I had to fight and threaten to turn myself in to the authorities if she wouldn't at least accept minimum wage and a place to stay. She's loaded. Her family, the assholes who abandoned her like just another thing they owned... Her full name is Cindi Renolt Middleton."

"Renolt?" He racked his brain. It couldn't be the same family he'd run across in his plans for the growth fund. "As in the oil magnate?"

"One and the same."

"If that's true, she's..."

"I did say *loaded*, didn't I, son?"

"Oh, fuck." Sam replayed the horror on her face and wished he could lash himself a hundred times for each of the heartbreakingly beautiful tears that had graced her cheeks last night. "Oh, holy fuck."

"Now you're catching on." JD grinned. "So what are you going to do about it?"

"I'll make it right. If she'll let me." Panic sent chills down his spine. "She has to, right?"

"You'd better be damn convincing. Take your time. Do this right. It's important and I think you're running out of chances." JD sighed. "She's coming up to the house for the shindig this morning."

"You're not supposed to know about that." Sam

bowed his head and rubbed the tension from his neck. "Act surprised."

"Always do." He chuckled.

"I gotta go. Think." Sam started to rise.

"Sam." JD stopped him with light pressure on his shoulder.

"Dad?" He glanced over, then away again, afraid he might give in to the prickling behind his eyes if he didn't escape soon.

"Bring in that piece of shit walker. After the announcements this morning, I'll use it. Just not with everyone watching. You'll be there, right? By my side?"

"Yeah. I won't let you fall. I promise." He hugged JD, then ambled toward the storage shed, letting his chores distract him as he stewed over the right way to win Cindi back.

He couldn't afford to lose her.

An hour or two later, most everything was in place. Sam prepared to take a shower and raid Vicky's garden for a bouquet of flowers when his phone buzzed insistently. He was surprised to see Sawyer's face appear on his phone's screen. He figured his twin would still be fucking following weeks of abstinence.

After wishing for this call, he considered stuffing the device back in his pocket. How much more could one man take in a day?

Sawyer required his full attention. Sam drew an enormous breath, then answered the call. "Hey, bro."

"Sam." Sawyer's coldness caught him unaware. His brother rarely lost his temper and this tone was a far cry from last night's friendlier one.

"What's up, man? Didn't expect to hear from you this early. Not since you were so busy."

"Yeah, that's me. The brother too fucking busy to come back to Wyoming."

Shit. Sawyer knew where Sam was. Weeks of guilt over keeping the secret of JD's illness from his brother crashed in on his head. "Sawyer, I can explain—"

"Tell you what," Sawyer interrupted. "Why don't you start with the part where you tell me what the fuck is going on with JD?"

Sam took a deep breath. "Sounds like you already know."

What Sam couldn't figure out was how.

"I want to hear it from you. The person who should've told me to begin with."

"JD forbade us to say anything to you." *Nice, Sam. Take the goddamn coward's way out.*

"And being the good little son, you did exactly what your daddy told you to do. Say the fucking words, Sam."

"It's cancer. JD's dying." Time to man up and pay the piper. He'd known all along Sawyer would be angry as hell when he realized they'd kept the truth from him. Sam, of all people, knew how much their silence would hurt his brother. "I'm sorry, Sawyer."

"I'm coming home. Tonight if I can swing it. If not, on the first available flight."

Sam swallowed the lump lodged in his throat. "I'll pick you up at the airport."

"No. I have a ride. I don't need any favors from you."

"God dammit, Sawyer, you've got to let me explain—"

Sawyer's anger cut through the line. "When I get there, I'm kicking your ass. Explain it to my knuckles. Might take a piece out of Silas's and Seth's hides for good measure. Share that message with them, will you?"

The phone disconnected before Sam could reply.

Sam hovered outside Cindi's office in the barn. She'd ducked out of the retirement party for JD the moment she'd finished delivering a heartfelt speech about home and family that had pummeled the bruises on Sam's heart. He'd fulfilled his promise to JD, staying by his side despite his father hissing at him to run after the gorgeous woman. Now that the crowd had dispersed, Tupperware containers full of leftovers in tow, Sam found himself pacing outside the office in the barn.

He substituted his opening line at least a dozen times before realizing nothing he said would make up for the destruction he'd wreaked last night. Maybe he should forget it. Walk away before either of them could get hurt.

Or hurt more.

From hand to hand, he tossed the screwdriver he'd snagged from one of the toolboxes in the shed when he'd read Colby's note on the fridge: *File cabinet jammed in Cindi's office. Needs it opened to finish ordering this afternoon. Take care of it? Thx, C.*

As if the universe could sense the one place he'd least like to step foot in. *Fuck.*

Before he could devise the greatest bunch of bullshit excuse of all time to wrap around himself like an asbestos suit against the flames of her mighty wrath, he caught a melody drifting from the office. He recognized it instantly.

Sam grabbed the broom leaning against the wall beside him and went with his instincts. If nothing else, making a fool of himself might lure her into a smile he definitely didn't deserve and could hardly find the balls to hope for. He got a running start, then trusted the hay-dust on hardwood to do the rest.

He skidded across the threshold into Cindi's

office, *Risky Business* style. With the broom-turned-microphone poised in front of his face, he performed a duet along with Sara Bareilles to "King of Anything".

Sophisticated? Nope.

Humble? Yep.

He kept going with his off-key rendition until Cindi yanked at the lavender tresses swirling around her perfect oval face. She opened her mouth and he covered her lips with his palm before she could order him out.

"Cin." He perched on her desk, afraid if he didn't he'd invade her space and scoop her into his arms. "I'm so sorry. I acted like a total ass last night. It's just that I had a shitty time of things before I left NY and with JD, well, I never really came to terms with all that happened, you know? That's no reason for me to assume you were like her. I just..."

"I want to throw your ass out. I've never been as angry at a man as I was at you last night." She sighed. "As I still am. How dare you accuse me? If you saw what you did and still thought what you did, I can't believe you'll ever really understand me."

Damn. He'd fucking blown it before *it* had really started.

"But...you make it impossible to stay mad." She gave him a wry grin. "That was ridiculous and adorable and, you're right, no man is the king of me. So if it's a crown you're looking for—"

"No, Cindi, it's not at all." He reached slowly for her shoulder, giving her time to shut him down.

She didn't.

Christ, her skin was so soft beneath the flutter sleeve of her delicate silk top. The pure, light material spoke of understated quality. *Focus, Sam!*

"In fact, that's sort of what I came here to say. I've gone over the books and studied up on the changes you've made since you came onboard."

She jumped in, her eyes glittering. "And now you think you can waltz in here with your flashy Columbia degree and do better? I'd like to see you try. I know my shit."

"Exactly." He refused to allow her to brush his fingers from her arm. He couldn't give up the warmth flowing through her and up his arm.

"What?"

"No matter what happens between us, I need you to know that I respect what you've done here. Your negotiations with the suppliers, the seasonal budgeting and aggressive process improvements have made a huge impact on the operation of the ranch. So, thank you. I hope you won't penalize my family because I acted like an asshole."

She stared at him with her mouth open. It made him remember the sinful things she'd done with those pretty lips and skilled pink tongue. No. Not yet. He had to finish what he'd started or he'd regret it later.

"JD told me about your...circumstances. I should have put it together. With Belinda. She recognized you, didn't she? Maybe from Sotheby's. She haunts the auctions, always looking to have something no one else can, and you had tons of artwork in the cottage. The sculptures and vases. She would know the movers and shakers. It's how she works."

This time there was no restraining her.

"What?" She shoved back from the desk and bolted to her feet. "JD had no right to do that. So all of this—your sudden faith, the apology, all of it—is because your dad told you I'm rich? Would you have kept on thinking I was a fucking whore if he hadn't opened his big mouth?"

Sam should have denied it, but he didn't care to lie to her.

Her adorable face crumpled before she turned

away.

His arms ached. He craved holding her so badly. Still, he realized his touch would do anything but alleviate the agony he'd inflicted. "Cindi."

"Enough, Sam. I thought I'd finally found someone who would chose me over money. Someone who knows the value of family and friends. A partner who shared my kinks, my need to be a part of something bigger than myself. Someone who could identify and enjoy and...damn it." She kicked the jammed filing cabinet that'd drawn him into her realm in the first place.

"I'm sorry." He couldn't think of anything else to say. "I'd like to be those things. If you'll let me try again. I can't unlearn what JD shared. What do you want me to do?"

"Fix this fucking drawer and get the hell out," she screeched at him, then clapped a hand over her mouth.

He lunged for her, unable to keep from soothing her a moment longer.

"Ow, fuck." He'd forgotten about the screwdriver jammed in his pocket and stood too fast, jabbing his leg. Probably warranted it too.

Cindi had retreated out of arm's reach. He sighed, then decided it might be best to do as she'd asked. He'd take care of the issue, then regroup. Staying here, pissing her off, would only do more damage.

Sam knelt by the side of the cabinet and tugged on the drawer handle. The edge near the lock bent in. Another solid yank yielded similar results. So he placed the tip of the flathead screwdriver near the seam and tried to realign the lock latch.

A tiny sniffle from Cindi's direction distracted him just as he shoved the tool into the gap between the frame and the door.

The sharp metal slipped, gouging the base of his

thumb. "Son of a bitch!"

He shook his hand until he realized the motion flung droplets of blood.

"Sam!" Cindi rushed over, giving him hope. She wasn't immune to his injury, not that the sting in his thumb held a candle to the wrenching of his heart.

"If you'd asked a real cowboy instead of a pansy MBA, you'd have a man in your drawers by now." Silas hobbled over to where they crouched on the floor.

Sam didn't say anything. He allowed Cindi to wrap a tissue around his hand and keep pressure on the wound. Well worth the discomfort.

Silas inspected the fixture for a moment or two, then thumped the side hard with his fist.

The fucking thing popped open.

"Show-off," Sam muttered.

Silas grinned, then angled for the door. "Still have the touch. Now, could you two keep it down in here? You're spooking the horses."

Cindi looked away, but Sam caught her chin in his good hand, his brother completely forgotten. "I'll go if you don't want to talk to me anymore. I only want to say one thing. I'm sorry. Truly. I care for you, Cindi. It's been a rollercoaster—"

"Zip it, Sam. You can blame our issues on bad timing, me fucking other guys, money, whatever is the *excuse du jour*. But it all comes down to one thing. You. You forgot how to trust. Or maybe you just don't want to take that chance again." She closed her eyes and sighed. "As much as I'd like to stay pissed off, I can't. I understand."

"You do?" He accepted her tender hug, soaking in empathy.

"Yeah." She nodded. "I'll miss you, Sam."

"What?" He blinked. "What just happened here?"

"Simply because I get you—totally—doesn't

mean I'll subject myself to an eternity of disappointment. I'm done with wasting my affection on people who can't say the same for me." Her eyes turned glassy as tears gathered. "My parents, so-called friends…you. I'm always the one left hurting when another person important to me smacks me in the face. I'm done with that shit. Leave. Or I will."

"No. Wait. I *do* understand you, Cindi." He couldn't catch his breath fast enough to explain.

"Really?" She cocked her hip and planted one hand on the seductive curve.

"Yes, I swear. We were meant for each other." He would have dropped to his knees and groveled if he wasn't already there. "I'll spend the rest of my life proving it to you if I have to. Just don't walk away. I get you. I won't let you down again."

"Then prove it." The firm set of her jaw made it clear she didn't believe him anymore. "One last chance. Take me on the perfect date tomorrow. *My* idea of perfect. Make me an offer I can't refuse and maybe I'll consider seeing you again."

He opened his mouth.

Closed it.

A slow, steady grin spread across his face. She had no idea what corner she'd negotiated herself into.

"You think this is funny?" She shook her head.

"I take my deals very seriously." When she would have given him her shoulder, he dipped in and stole a kiss to tide him over. Her brief hesitation gave him hope. "I never miss out on a bargain. Especially not one as sweet as this. See you tomorrow, Cindi."

Chapter Sixteen

Sam silently apologized to Dee for the flowers braided into her mane. Lucy had done the same for Cindi's mount after she'd listened to his plan. Jody had helped him gather supplies, both women sure he could convince the wild bookkeeper to forgive him. Maybe more.

Cindi had been quiet when he picked her up from the barn in his favorite Brioni shirt and Lucky jeans. Though she'd allowed him to kiss her hello, the passion of the other night had been missing. Of course, he'd loitered until the sparks neither of them could deny reignited.

That had only seemed to piss her off more, though.

As they'd wandered across the land together, the firm set of her shoulders had relaxed. He told her stories of his youth, including silly things he'd done with his brothers here. Serious things too. Like his recounting of the night before Silas left for Alaska. He drew her into the fabric of his home as much as he could, inviting her to take what she'd missed and be part of his future.

They walked their mounts up the final rocky incline before the ridge. The same one he'd shown her from the lookout last month. God, it seemed like years ago.

Sam measured the sun as it dipped toward the horizon, then clicked his tongue against the roof of his mouth. They had to pick up the pace a little if his surprise was going to be perfect.

For Cindi he would settle for nothing less.

She wouldn't accept half-assed anymore. He didn't blame her.

He'd spent the day debating how grand of a gesture to make. When he'd shared his thoughts with JD, his father had wholeheartedly approved of taking an enormous leap. If nothing else, the smile on JD's face had been worth potential rejection.

Now, you're talking, son. There's the Sammy I know and love. Bet big. Win big.

Or lose epically.

The top of the tent he'd pitched earlier came into view along with a gorgeous picnic spread made of the finest ingredients he could rummage up on short notice. He'd gotten a speeding ticket racing into Laramie for essentials like Beluga caviar and Rogue Creamery Blue Vein cheese to go with the bottle of Cristal chilling in the cheap red plastic cooler.

If his outing made Cindi smile, he'd pay the damn thing gladly.

Paper lanterns covered electric bulbs running off a mini-generator Colby had dragged out of storage. Although the sun still shone, soon the lights would illuminate their perch. The path was scattered with more flowers and led to the open flap of the canvas tent, which sheltered a cheap air mattress covered in fine linens.

The blend of extravagant and practical had

seemed perfect when he arranged them. Cindi didn't say a single word as Sam tied their horses. He grew nervous as he prepared to turn around and weigh her reaction.

Cindi had stopped dead in her tracks, her gaze flitting from one thing to another. Fresh fruit overflowed silver dishes and color splashed from roses set in vases ringing their getaway.

"Is this lame? I could have chartered a jet into Vegas or LA. Hell, France if you wanted the real deal. We could leave right now." Sam would have promised her the world, but she covered his lips with her fingers.

"I'm exactly where I want to be." She kissed him tenderly, then drew him down onto the thick cashmere blanket he'd set out on top of the air mattress and held down with rocks from around the campsite. "I don't need anything other than what's right here. This is amazing. All my favorite foods. You listened to me when we talked. Remembered. It matters to you. That's all I hoped for."

"Glad to hear it." He nuzzled their noses. "'Cause there's pretty much nothing I can give you that you couldn't get for yourself. Do you know how much that sucks?"

Fuck, he wished he could lavish his woman with impressive shit, and she already had more than he could provide.

"Maybe you still don't understand?" She climbed to her knees, putting her palm flat on his chest so he couldn't follow.

"I think I've fucked up enough for one week." He grimaced. "Why don't you explain it? Real slow. Simple even."

Laughter fell from her lips at that. "You're no dummy, Sam Compton. You just act like one sometimes."

The truth stung.

"I really l-like all those things about you. You're smart, funny, sophisticated and yet not pompous. You recognize quality but aren't enchanted by overpriced bullshit with a fancy name."

He nodded. So far so good.

Then she knocked his elbow from beneath him and straddled his waist. Unlike Belinda, she didn't attempt to smack sense into him. It might have hurt less if she had. "When will you realize you already have the most valuable thing in the world? Your family. Their undying love and the blood bond that goes deeper than any other tie. That's priceless."

"I'm sorry to have to respectfully disagree with you." He flipped them, rotating until he pressed her into the cloud of air pillowing them from the stones below.

He stole a kiss before continuing, just in case she kicked his ass out. Because he couldn't hide his feelings from her for one more minute.

When it's time, you'll know. Tell her the truth. Tell her how it all started. You can have this. She can, too. Vicky's advice echoed in his mind. She'd held JD's hand as they gave their blessing over his plan for the evening.

"There's a bond stronger than blood." He traced her eyebrow with his thumb.

"It sure as hell isn't money or fame or power."

"No." He took a deep breath. "It's love."

She blinked up at him.

"The kind that JD and Vicky have. Or Colby, Si and Lucy. Or Seth and Jody. You can't buy that. It's where blood bonds come from. They're a product of that magic. And that's where you've been missing the point, Cin." He cupped her shoulders but resisted shaking her. "You don't have to be born into the perfect family. You can make one yourself. If you meet the right person."

She blinked up at him. "H-have you met the right person?"

"Hell, yes." He closed his eyes, afraid to ask. Her breasts pressed against his chest as his breaths came quick and hard. His heart skipped a beat or three. "Have you?"

"From the first moment I saw you, I knew." Her fingers shook when she touched his cheek. "Every day I spent at Compass Ranch, it was you I was waiting for."

"I'm glad you had the other cowboys to keep you company until now." He tickled her until she dissolved into a fit of giggles. While she was distracted, he slipped something from his pocket. He peered over his shoulder as the rays of the sun bronzed her regal cheekbones in their golden glow. Then he untangled their limbs and scooted toward the edge of the mattress.

"Sam?" She bit her lip. "I meant that, you know. It wasn't a joke."

"I'm not kidding either." He grabbed her ankles and tugged until she perched on the edge of their makeshift bed while he knelt on the ground in the spot he hoped to remember fondly for the rest of his life. "How's this for serious?"

The diamonds in his great aunt Meade's antique ring sparkled in the sunset.

"What are you doing?" She put her hand over her open mouth.

"I'm asking you if you'll share the only really priceless thing I own. Help me make something even more wonderful." He took her hand in his and poised the ring at the tip of her third finger. "Will you take my name? Our name? Make it official. Marry me and be a Compton for life?"

"I—" She shook her head. "I don't want to be a Compton."

"You don't?" His eyes went wide. He'd been so damn sure...

"No." She swiped a tear from her lashes. "I love your family and this place with all my heart. I do. But, Sam, I want to belong to *you*. No matter what your name is. You're right. Together, we'll build a future."

"Thank God." It took two tries to slip the ring on her finger. A perfect fit. "Because you already own my soul."

"Is that what the kids are calling it these days?" She winked.

He laughed and tackled her. They bounced together, bathed in a deepening amber flare of light. "You can call it whatever you like, especially when I'm showing my wife off to the hands."

"You wouldn't mind if we—"

"Hell, no. I love you, Cindi." His hand snaked beneath her blouse as he kissed her. The smooth caress of her bare skin on his grounded him. "Exactly the way you are. I would never try to change what you like. In this case, I enjoy it too, you know?"

"I did notice that." She grinned. "And I love you too. Sam?"

"Yes?" He forced himself to pause in his exploration of her neck long enough to meet her serious stare.

"I've never been more positive. I'm the most fortunate woman in the world."

"And it's only going to get better from here." He slid his hand toward her mound. "Would you like me to show you how?"

"Please, do." She moaned and wrapped her legs around his waist, hugging him tight. "Please."

This time, the night Sam spent on the ridge wasn't focused on the end of an era, but the beginning of one.

What Happens Next?

If you've enjoyed the Compass Brothers so far, don't wait to find out what happens to them next in Western Ties.

How strong are the ties that bind?

Leah Hollister's sex life needs a swift kick in the pants. Small-town Compton Pass, though, isn't the place to explore her need for bondage. When she gets an invitation to a BDSM party out in LA, she wastes no time booking a flight.

Her plan to play anonymously is shot to hell when she runs into high-school crush Sawyer Compton—and he lays immediate claim to her.

Sawyer Compton commands total control, in and out of the bedroom. He never thought Leah could handle his darker urges, but one look at the white bracelet that marks her as a sub ripe for the picking, and he knows exactly how this night is going to end. With Leah in his bed.

Leah didn't expect to enjoy the comfort Sawyer's familiarity brings, even as his touch takes her to unimaginable heights of pleasure. When bad news from home sends him reeling, she's more than prepared to offer him anything he needs: her body, her friendship. Even her heart—if Sawyer can loosen the reins over his own to accept her love.

Warning: Invest in tissues. Lots and lots of tissues. Between spicy, set-the-sheets-on-fire bondage romps and the last Compass brother coming home, you'll need them.

An Excerpt From Western Ties:

"Leah?" a familiar male voice behind her said.

Leah closed her eyes and prayed she'd imagined it. There was no way. No possible way—

"Leah Hollister?"

She sighed. Fuck. What were the chances?

Turning, she realized her night wasn't going to end as she'd planned. She should have saved her money. Should have stayed in Compton Pass. She was screwed.

"Sawyer." She didn't bother with the pretense of being happy to see him. "What the hell are you doing here?"

"Leah," Stacey whispered, her voice full of warning.

Sawyer narrowed his eyes, refusing to answer. His gaze started at the top, taking in her dramatic makeup, before drifting lower to her breasts, accentuated by the tight corset Stacey had loaned her. She willed herself to remain still as he finished his visual tour with a long look at her short leather skirt and stocking-clad legs.

"Enjoying the view?" she taunted. "You still haven't answered my question. Shouldn't you be in San Francisco? What are you doing here?"

He scowled. "That's my question for you. A BDSM party in L.A. is a long way from a kindergarten classroom in Compton Pass. Last time I saw you, you were leading a pack of five-year-olds around my family's ranch."

223

A couple of years earlier, Sawyer had helped her organize a field trip to Compass ranch. It had been one of the highlights of the year for her students—and for her. It was also the last time she'd seen Sawyer. Two years was a long time. She certainly hadn't expected their reunion to take place in L.A.

She sucked in a deep breath and tried to hide her disappointment. He was right. She'd purposely put herself as far away from home as possible, so that she could indulge in these two nights. One weekend to confirm a few suspicions she'd always held in regard to her sexual preferences. Sawyer was going to put a wrench in the works.

She gestured at her outfit. "I would think my role here would be obvious." For the first time, she allowed her gaze to travel over him as well. Her body heated with arousal as she noted how unbelievably sexy he was. He wore tight dark jeans and a black T-shirt that hugged his muscular chest to perfection. No one in the place would fail to read the dominance in his stance, the aura of power he projected.

On the surface, she was shocked to find her friend in a place like this, but there was another part—deep inside—that wasn't a bit surprised. He belonged here.

"So you're a Dom?" She fought the urge to laugh as she asked the absurd question. Of course he was.

His gaze drifted to her arm. He grasped her wrist, pulling it up and toying with the white wristband the host had given her upon arrival.

"You understand what this means, right?" he asked, gesturing to the bracelet.

Sawyer completely ignored her Dom question. It didn't matter anyway. It had clearly been rhetorical. He was a Compton. Anybody and everybody from their neck of the woods knew that name was synonymous with alpha male.

She gave him an annoyed look. "Of course I do."

It was evident from his tone he didn't think she belonged here any more than Stacey. One of the reasons she'd planned this adventure far away from home, surrounded by strangers who didn't know her, was because rumors spread like wildfire in their small hometown. She knew about Sawyer's sexual proclivities, and she'd always wondered if she shared a few of them.

Besides, her *sweet* disposition didn't inspire the more adventurous cowboys back home to ask her out, so her opportunities for exploration were seriously limited. Stacey was right. She *was* a goody-goody.

Sawyer didn't appear to like her answer, so he restated the obvious. "It means you are an unattached submissive who's looking for a Dom. This wristband has declared it open season on you."

She shrugged, unconcerned. "Sorry to shatter the illusion, Sawyer, but I think I can handle whatever this party dishes out. It's not like I'm a virgin."

He frowned. "You lost your virginity in the backseat of a Pontiac to Les Prescott after Compton Pass won the district football championship our senior year. The guy was a shithead. You should've chosen better."

Leah laughed, though a ripple of desire slammed into her. It was always this way with Sawyer. Though they were just friends, there'd never been a time when she hadn't felt his gaze on her. He'd scared off more than a few would-be boyfriends in her lifetime claiming they were *only after one thing*. Les had fallen into that category, but Sawyer had been playing on that championship team and had been a bit distracted that night.

Sawyer had appointed himself her personal guardian in third grade when Jordan Haskiell had shoved her down on the playground after she'd beat him in a footrace. As a result, Sawyer had endured an afternoon in the principal's office and God only knew what kind of punishment at home after issuing Jordan a very physical, very painful warning of what happened to guys who messed with Leah. While Sawyer hadn't pursued her romantically, he'd certainly taken the bonds of friendship to a new extreme.

Despite the fact they'd existed in different cliques at school, Sawyer hadn't let social status stop him from being one of her best friends. He'd run with the jocks and cheerleaders, while she'd been firmly encamped with the brainiacs, less affectionately referred to as nerds by their peers. "How could you have known about Les?"

"I told you. He was a prick. He was bragging about it at school the following Monday."

She flushed. She'd never heard of Les spreading rumors about her. "I didn't know—"

Sawyer grinned. "Luckily, he started his boasting with me. I took him out behind the school and gave him a reason to shut his fucking mouth."

His admission held a hint of humor, but she could tell he was angry. She decided to test the waters to see how screwed she was.

"Well, it was great to see you again, but Stacey and I were going to pop over to the bar for a drink."

"I'll go with you." He confirmed her fear.

She smiled and shook her head. "No, I don't think that's a good idea. You're scaring off all the other Doms."

His wolfish grin let her know that was his intent.

Her temper sparked. "God dammit, Sawyer. Go away."

Stacey lightly touched her arm, alerting Leah that she'd spoken too loudly. Several people glanced in her direction and frowned. She was never going to achieve her goal at this rate.

Sawyer was the only person in the room who didn't take offense at her faux pas. "You realize this is a weekend party?"

She nodded. It was starting to look like it would be a long two days.

Sawyer reclaimed her hand, slipping off the white bracelet.

"What the hell are you doing?" She tried to pull her arm free, attempting to grab the wristband back.

Sawyer's grip was implacable. He reached into his pocket and pulled out a green bracelet. Suddenly, she felt dizzy. There was no way he would—

Sawyer slipped it around her wrist.

"No," she whispered when he lifted her hand.

About the Authors

Jayne Rylon and Mari Carr met at a writing conference in June 2009 and instantly became arch enemies. Two authors couldn't be more opposite. Mari, when free of her librarian-by-day alter ego, enjoys a drink or two or... more. Jayne, allergic to alcohol, lost huge sections her financial-analyst mind to an epic explosion resulting from Mari gloating about her hatred of math. To top it off, they both had works in progress with similar titles and their heroes shared a name. One of them would have to go.

The battle between them for dominance was a bloody, but short one, when they realized they'd be better off combining their forces for good (or smut). With the ink dry on the peace treaty, they emerged as good friends, who have a remarkable amount in common despite their differences, and their writing partnership has flourished. Except for the time Mari attempted to poison Jayne with a bottle of Patron. Accident or retaliation? You decide.

Join Mari's newsletter and Jayne's Naughty News so you don't miss new releases, contests, or exclusive subscriber-only content.

Also by Jayne Rylon

MEN IN BLUE
Hot Cops Save Women In Danger
Night is Darkest
Razor's Edge
Mistress's Master
Spread Your Wings
Wounded Hearts
Bound For You

DIVEMASTERS
Sexy SCUBA Instructors By Day, Doms On A Mega-Yacht By Night
Going Down
Going Deep
Going Hard

POWERTOOLS
Five Guys Who Get It On With Each Other & One Girl. Enough Said?
Kate's Crew
Morgan's Surprise
Kayla's Gift
Devon's Pair
Nailed to the Wall
Hammer it Home

HOT RODS
Powertools Spin Off. Keep up with the Crew Seven Guys & One Girl. Enough Said?
King Cobra
Mustang Sally
Super Nova
Rebel on the Run

Swinger Style
Barracuda's Heart
Touch of Amber
Long Time Coming

STANDALONE
Menage
4-Ever Theirs
Nice & Naughty
Contemporary
Where There's Smoke
Report For Booty

COMPASS BROTHERS
Modern Western Family Drama Plus Lots Of Steamy Sex
Northern Exposure
Southern Comfort
Eastern Ambitions
Western Ties

COMPASS GIRLS
Daughters Of The Compass Brothers Drive Their Dads Crazy And Fall In Love
Winter's Thaw
Hope Springs
Summer Fling
Falling Softly

PLAY DOCTOR
Naughty Sexual Psychology Experiments
Dream Machine
Healing Touch

RED LIGHT
A Hooker Who Loves Her Job

Complete Red Light Series Boxset
FREE - Through My Window - FREE
Star
Can't Buy Love
Free For All

PICK YOUR PLEASURES
Choose Your Own Adventure Romances!
Pick Your Pleasure
Pick Your Pleasure 2

RACING FOR LOVE
MMF Menages With Race-Car Driver Heroes
Complete Series Boxset
Driven
Shifting Gears

PARANORMALS
Vampires, Witches, And A Man Trapped In A Painting
Paranormal Double Pack Boxset
Picture Perfect
Reborn

Look for these titles by Mari Carr

Big Easy
Blank Canvas
Crash Point
Full Position
Rough Draft
Triple Beat
Winner Takes All
Going Too Fast

Boys of Fall:
Free Agent
Red Zone
Wild Card

Compass:
Northern Exposure
Southern Comfort
Eastern Ambitions
Western Ties
Winter's Thaw
Hope Springs
Summer Fling
Falling Softly

Farepoint Creek:
Outback Princess
Outback Cowboy
Outback Master
Outback Lovers

June Girls:
No Recourse
No Regrets

Just Because:
Because of You
Because You Love Me
Because It's True

Lowell High:
Bound by the Past
Covert Affairs
Mad about Meg

Bundles
Cowboy Heat
Sugar and Spice

Madison Girls
Scoundrels

Second Chances:
Fix You
Dare You
Just You
Near You
Reach You
Always You

Sparks in Texas:
Sparks Fly
Waiting for You
Something Sparked
Off Limits
No Other Way
Whiskey Eyes

Trinity Masters:
Elemental Pleasure
Primal Passion
Scorching Desire
Forbidden Legacy
Hidden Devotion
Elegant Seduction
Secret Scandal
Delicate Ties

Wild Irish:
Come Monday
Ruby Tuesday
Waiting for Wednesday
Sweet Thursday
Friday I'm in Love
Saturday Night Special
Any Given Sunday
Wild Irish Christmas
January Girl
February Stars

Individual Titles:
Seducing the Boss
Tequila Truth
Erotic Research
Rough Cut
Happy Hour

Power Play
One Daring Night
Assume the Positions
Slam Dunk

What Was Your Favorite Part?

Did you enjoy this book? If so, please leave a review and tell your friends about it. Word of mouth and online reviews are immensely helpful and greatly appreciated.

Jayne's Shop

Check out Jayne's online shop for autographed print books, direct download ebooks, reading-themed apparel up to size 5XL, mugs, tote bags, notebooks, Mr. Rylon's wood (you'll have to see it for yourself!) and more.

www.jaynerylon.com/shop

Listen Up!

The majority of Jayne's books are also available in audio format on Audible, Amazon and iTunes.